Days of Future Past

Part III - Future Tense

Published by John Van Stry
Copyright 2017 John Van Stry

Copyright John Van Stry 2017
Cover Credits: eBook Launch (http://ebooklaunch.com/)

No part of this Book may be reproduced in any form without expressed, written consent from the author.

Any resemblance between characters in this story and people living or dead is purely coincidental. Any resemblance between places, locations, organizations, companies, things, imagined or actual is also purely coincidental. This is a work of fiction created by the author and the author retains all rights to the material in this story.

P064106b
ISBN-13: 978-1979716840

ISBN-10: 1979716846

Days of Future Past Trilogy:
Past Tense
Present Tense
Future Tense

Hammer Commission Series:
The Hammer Commission
The King of Las Vegas
Wolf Killer
Loose Ends

Portals of Infinity Series:
Portals of Infinity: Champion for Hire
Portals of Infinity: The God Game
Portals of Infinity: Of Temples and Trials
Portals of Infinity: The Sea of Grass
Portals of Infinity: Demigod and Deities
Portals of Infinity: Reprisal
Portals of Infinity: Kaiju

I would like to thank the following people for their support:

Andrew Waters via Patreon

Chad Glidden for his support with everything else

- 1 -

I yawned and rolled over on my side to watch Sarah and Heather as they swam and played in the pond, enjoying the view rather shamelessly as neither one of them was wearing anything.

"What are you smiling at?" Heather asked, grinning at me.

"My wives," I grinned back.

She laughed and went back to cavorting with Sarah; neither of them was shy about showing their own feelings for each other. But then they weren't shy about showing those feelings to me either.

I think I was finally getting used to the idea that not only was I married, but I was married to two women who loved me as much as they loved each other.

The last several weeks had actually been rather pleasant. Coyote had steered us to a forgotten small town that was once known as Paradise Valley, in northern Nevada. It was forgotten because of the destruction caused by the 'yellow volcano' the top of which you could actually see off to the northeast, if you were standing up on one of the nearby mountain tops.

According to Sarah, when the volcano blew, which apparently happened during the big slam, it destroyed everything within a couple hundred miles. Either by shockwave, falling rocks, poisonous gases, lava, or all the glaciers on top of all the hills melting almost instantly.

I got out a map after she told me this and she pointed at what had once been Yellowstone National Park. Now it was a massive volcano and most of Idaho had been devastated, along with a lot of Wyoming, Montana, and parts of northern Utah and Nevada. Apparently the destruction went as far as eastern Oregon and the western half of both of the Dakotas. The 'Nev Wastes' was pretty much a name for everything to the south and west of the volcano now.

But stuck in this valley, this town had survived, sort of. A rather large bolder had landed in the middle of town, and by large I mean about the size of a football field. It had leveled just about everything in town as well as dammed the small stream coming through, which had created the pond the girls were now using.

We'd found a nice place to stay, just outside of the remains of the town. It looked like it had once been a ranch of some sort; most of the buildings had fallen down ages ago. But the main house had a rather well built cellar that had included a concrete roof. I don't know if the builder had been a survivalist, or just liked to overbuild things, but in either case, we had a nice dry and secure place to sleep.

"I need you to leave tomorrow."

I sat up and looked over to my left. Sure enough, there was Coyote.

"Why hello to you too," I sighed.

"What? No, 'thank you for the vacation, Coyote?'" he said, smirking at me.

I grinned back at him, "My parents didn't teach me any manners. What's your excuse?"

"Why, I didn't have any parents of course," he said and gave one of those little bark-laughs of his.

"Well, I do appreciate the rest," I told him. "So where are we off to next?"

"I need you to deal with a small problem, which means heading to a relay station a couple of days travel to the east of here."

"A relay station?" I asked, a bit curious.

"Aybem uses it to communicate with some of his resources, as well as a few of the forestry and weather satellites that have managed to survive in orbit. It's the least important one; he has several after all, so it should be lightly guarded."

"What does Aybem need weather satellites for?"

"Riggs has his army getting ready to march off to Aybem's stronghold. Once he gets going, it should take him about ten days to get there and meet up with the armies of the Cheyenne, Apache, and Ute tribes. The forestry and weather satellites make it possible for Aybem to track Riggs' forces and deploy ambushes and counterattacks.

"By removing this little bit of intelligence gathering, it will make it much easier for Riggs to gather his armies around Aybem's stronghold."

I nodded, it made sense.

"Okay, so we go to this relay station, and then what?"

"I'll tell you want you need to do, once you get there. But without the satellites, Aybem won't really know where Riggs' forces are, until they've laid siege to him, as Riggs prepares his final assault."

"And then what? I'm guessing you have another job for me to take care of during Riggs' siege?"

"Your job, plain and simple is to make sure that Riggs does not fail."

I shook my head, "I don't see how I'm going to be able to do that. First off, Riggs and I don't really get along all that well. Hell, I think Heather has plans on shooting him the next time she sees him."

"Not unlike her plans to shoot me?" Coyote snickered.

I glanced over at the pond, Sarah had Heather pretty well distracted. I don't know if that was because she noticed Coyote was here, or just because she liked abusing Heather.

"I think Heather may forgive you, now that we've had some time off," I chuckled. "But," I said returning to my original point, "how am I supposed to make sure he succeeds? I can't command his armies if he dies. Not that I could do anywhere near as a good a job with them as he can."

"Paul, this isn't about winning the battle at Aybem's stronghold. It's about going inside his lair and killing him. *That* is the goal of all of this. Aybem isn't going to come out, ever. Someone has to go inside and destroy him. Riggs knows that, and now you know it too."

"So you want me to go into his lair," I paused a moment, "why the hell do they always call it a lair?" I grumbled at that. "And kill some big powerful, what? Warlord? Mage? Demon? Just what the *hell* is this guy anyways?"

"Yes, all of that. And well, if I called it his office, you wouldn't take it seriously, now would you?" Coyote said with a smirk.

"So just how am I supposed to get by all of Riggs' army, Aybem's army, and make my way into his 'lair'?"

"Why, by sneaking in of course."

"Ha, ha. Very funny. I don't think dressing up in a western union outfit and trying to deliver a candygram is going to work all that well."

"Ah, but I know something that neither Riggs, nor Aybem knows."

"And that would be?"

"Aybem's lair is in the hills to the east of the old spaceport. Hills that are riddled with tunnels from when they mined copper and gold there."

I sat up straight and stared at him.

"Did you say *spaceport*?"

"Yes. The mines you want are to the west of Ruth, south of highway fifty. The remains of the spaceport are about fifteen miles east of that, on the other side of the hills."

"They had spaceports?" I said, still staring at him.

Coyote nodded, "Yes, they had spaceports. And space travel, space stations, Moon bases and all of that."

"Interstellar flight?" I prodded him.

Coyote shook his head, "No, just ships within the solar system. And it wasn't very fast."

"Hey! Fleabag! What are you doing here!!" I heard Heather yell.

"And that would be my cue," Coyote grinned and I turned to see Heather raising a rifle, stark naked and dripping wet. Damn if she didn't look good like that.

"Heather!" Sarah was laughing.

"Dammit! He disappeared on me!"

I shook my head and sighed.

"So, does this mean we are leaving?" Sarah asked, coming over to where I was sitting and picking up a towel. She looked good dripping wet as well.

"Tomorrow," I nodded. "You never told me they had spaceflight before the war."

Sarah shrugged and dried off. "There is not a lot of history on it. There were a lot of people who did not like it, supposedly, and there was some kind of labor dispute. I think there was even a strike or something involving it. But then the big slam came and everyone was so busy trying to survive that disaster that I guess nothing more was ever written down about it."

"So what happened to everyone? In space that is?"

Sarah shrugged, "No one knows. Or if they do, they are not talking. I would guess either they came back here, or died up there."

I shook my head and thought about that. Space travel. Not just a couple of trips to the Moon and then giving up, like back in the early seventies before I was born, but regular travel, with bases on the Moon and all that stuff.

"I wonder if there are any rockets left?"

"After all these years?" Sarah shook her head and picked up her clothes, "I doubt it, and even if any did survive, what kind of shape would they be in?"

"What are you two talking about?" Heather asked coming over.

"Space travel," I told her. "I had no idea it had gotten so big."

Heather shrugged, "Eh, I'm not much for ancient history. So what does our task master want now?"

"Riggs is preparing to march on Aybem. So it's time for us to go and help him out, and for me to make sure that Riggs kills him."

"That'll be quite the trick."

"Huh?"

"He's supposed to be what, two hundred years old? Sarah?" Heather asked looking at Sarah who had put her pants on, but had left her top off.

"At least three," Sarah said. "No one really knows just how old he is."

"What is he?" I asked, "An elf?"

Sarah shook her head, "No one really seems to know. The stories from the orcs and others who have been captured make him out to be something different. Some people think he is a demon or the like. He is like ten feet tall, has skin like stone and a crown of snakes or some such thing."

"Coyote told me he never leaves his lair?"

"If it is his place of power, he won't leave it while under attack. But none of the stories we have ever heard say he can not leave it," Sarah shrugged again. "Back when he was first encountered, it was while leading orcish armies across the wastes to conquer or drive out the other factions."

"Well, I woulda asked more questions," I turned and looked at Heather, "but someone didn't give me the chance."

Heather blushed all the way down to her navel and looked a little embarrassed as she got dressed.

"Okay, Okay, I promise not to shoot the flea bag anymore."

"And don't go shooting Riggs either," I warned.

"Not until after he has killed Aybem at least," Sarah added with a smile.

- 2 -

I was lying prone just behind the hilltop, looking over it at a small light brown concrete building just below the summit of the next mountain over. There was an antenna tower on the top of the mountain, with a number of microwave dishes on it, and several other antennas coming off the top and sides of the tower.

Most of the microwave dishes looked to be damaged, and a couple of what I guess were antenna mounts looked like some of the antennas that had once been on it were missing now as well.

"What the hell is that place?" Heather asked, looking at it through the scope on her rifle.

"Coyote says it's a relay station and it's being used by Aybem," I replied, studying it through my binoculars.

"What else did he say?"

"Not much, as you were about to shoot at him before I could question him any further," I chuckled.

Heather scowled and tried not to look embarrassed.

"So, he wants you to go in there?" Sarah asked, also looking at the small building through her binoculars.

"Apparently, yes, he does."

"Well, it must be important, because there are guards stationed by it, and a camp farther down the mountain side."

"It can't be too important," Heather replied, "I only see two guards by the building and I suspect less than a dozen in the camp below."

"It's important," I told them as I steered my binoculars back down towards the camp.

"But Aybem has several of these; this one is just a backup."

The camp, when I found it, was about a third of the way down the mountain from the top, situated on the dirt road that led to the top. A road that got considerably narrower the closer to the top it went. The camp also had only two guards on duty, but considering the location and the surrounding terrain, I doubted they needed any more than that.

"More likely the guards are to ward off any locals who come to scavenge," Sarah said putting away her binoculars and sliding back down the hillside a few feet. "We are fairly deep in the Nev Wastes here, so it is not like they would have to worry about any real attacks."

"Good point," I agreed. "So, what do we do?"

"Kill 'em all," Heather said.

"How?" I asked as Sarah just grinned and rolled her eyes.

"Well normally I'd say to pick them off from here," Heather started, "but the wind down the valleys between these ridgelines and hilltops can be pretty squirrelly, so at this distance I'd probably miss."

I looked at Sarah.

"They are beyond the range of my magic; we will have to get closer."

I nodded and started to move backwards out of sight of the camp, "I suspected as much. I guess we'll just have to sneak up there tonight under cover of darkness and take them out."

"We might as well go have an early dinner and get some sleep before the sun goes down," Heather said, backing down from the top as both Sarah and I eyed her butt.

"Oh, definitely, I like the idea of going to bed early," Sarah teased and Heather scowled again, only she was blushing now as well.

"Definitely bed," I agreed and Sarah laughed, as Heather blushed even deeper.

We waited until midnight. Then after Sarah had cast spells on each of us to improve our night vision, we headed out.

Moving from where we had set up our camp to the base of the mountain that the relay station was on took at least an hour. Once there we spent a few minutes looking for a good spot to leave our horses, which we had been leading rather than riding through the darkness. Horses and extra gear secured, we then started up the dirt path to the camp. According to my watch it was almost three-thirty in the morning when we finally came to the last bend on the path before we'd come into sight of their lookouts.

"This late at night, I doubt they'll see us," Heather whispered on the radio and in my ear. "Orcs don't have the best night vision, but don't take any chances; they may have night scopes or a see in the dark spell."

I nodded my agreement and we started our way directly up the hillside, leaving the road. The plan was to come around on the camp from the west, rather than continuing up the dirt road, which approached from the east after a switchback where the main guard post was. So once we'd gone up another couple hundred feet, we turned to our right and started to carefully move through the scrub.

When the orc camp was just starting to come into sight we stopped and checked our weapons. Heather would move up and around until she had a good line of sight on the camp. Once she was in position she would signal us over our radios, then Sarah and I would head into camp, me leading.

Heather would then snipe the guards, after which Sarah and I would move from tent to tent and kill the others while they slept.

Sure, that wasn't fair, but fair can get you killed. Besides, they're orcs, who cares?

Ten minutes after Heather moved out I heard a click in my headset, and I started around into the camp. I heard several muted 'whooshes' as Heather's bullets flew by, as well as one loud grunt, but that was it.

"Guards are down," Heather whispered into my ear over the radio.

I looked around the camp, there were four tents.

I approached the first one and as Sarah pulled the flap open, I stepped inside.

Six cots, three to a side, all occupied, all asleep.

I looked back at Sarah, who came in behind me and we each took up a position between the heads of the first two cots. I looked down at the orc sleeping there and realized that it's one thing to say you're going to shoot someone dead in their sleep, but another entirely to do it. This wasn't in the head of battle, this was cold blood. Sure it was the enemy but....

I heard a soft thump followed by a wet smack, then another. I glanced over at Sarah, she'd already killed the first two and was now aiming at the third one in the next cot over.

I heard a noise and the one in front of me was stirring! Panicking I shot him in the head twice, then turning around I did the same for the one right there, and raising my rifle to shoot the third one I saw his head explode as he started to sit up and look around.

"Be a little faster next time, Hon," Sarah's voice whispered over the radio.

I nodded and led the way out of the tent feeling both embarrassed and just a little bit ashamed. There was a war on, they were the enemy, and neither side believed in quarter, prisoners, or anything but killing the other. I needed to remember that.

The next tent was the mess tent, and there were only two cots in it. The cooks I guess, and we each shot one and moved back outside.

The third tent, was another barracks tent, only this one had only three of the six cots occupied. I made fast work of the three sleepers before Sarah even got inside. The last thing I wanted was for her to think I couldn't do the job.

This was kind of stupid when I thought about all of the things I'd done so far, and how much I'd had to pay with my own blood for most of them. Still, they'd grown up here in this world that was so much tougher and crueler than the one I'd been raised in, so it wasn't any surprise to me that they were having an easier time of it when it came to cold-blooded killing.

The last tent was a little bigger than the others; there were the six cots, of which two were empty. But there was a separate section to the back. My guess was that the commander was in there.

I had just finished with the one on my side, when the tent flap to the back opened and looking up I saw a rather large orc standing there, naked, and scratching himself as he yawned.

I brought my rifle up and pointed at him just as his mouth snapped shut and his eyes got wide as he saw me standing there as Sarah finished off the last of his men with another quiet shot.

I put two in his head as he opened his mouth to yell something, and then another two in his body as he hadn't even started to fall over yet.

Running to the back of the tent as his body started to slowly fall forward I went around him and pointing my rifle barrel at his cot I put four more shots into the lump I saw there.

"What is in there?" Sarah commed me from out in the larger area.

"Single cot, I think there may have been another body in it, so I put a few rounds into it."

"Better safe than sorry," Sarah agreed.

Using the muzzle of my rifle I pulled the blanket off the bed to see what was there.

It was a girl.

"Oh, shit!" I swore.

"You okay, Paul?" Sarah's voice came over the radio as I looked at the body.

She was young, or had been before I'd shot her. Two of my shots had hit her, one in the chest, which was probably instantly fatal, the other in her left arm, which it had severed from her body.

"Paul!" Sarah growled over the radio.

"I'm, I'm okay," I said, staring down at the dead body. She was dirty, and she was thin, she'd been what? I'd have guessed fourteen, maybe fifteen?

And I shot her. Dead.

"There was a girl in the bed."

"What?"

I looked up to see Sarah standing at the entryway in to the back area.

"She's dead, I killed her," I said, and pushing past her I went outside to get some fresh air and get away from the smell of filth, blood, and excrement.

Dropping to my knees I bent over and took deep breaths. I'd killed an innocent, a civilian. Hell, more like I'd killed some poor slave who'd been getting raped every night and who knows what other hell she'd been going through.

"You okay, Hon?" Heather's voice came over the radio.

"I, I'm not sure," I replied.

"He killed a girl who was in the boss's bed," Sarah came over the radio.

"I heard," Heather sighed. "Fortunes of war, Hon. I'm sorry. She's better off now."

"But I don't know that!" I growled back, trying to keep my voice down, but angry at what I'd done all the same.

"I do," Heather replied softly. "I've seen it before, they don't treat these girls well, Paul. Sooner or later, they kill them. They're nothing to the orcs. They treat their pets better."

"I, I don't know," I sighed.

Sarah put an arm around me as she squatted down next to me, "You didn't know, Hon. How could you? And what if she had woken up and screamed or yelled? The two up the hill would know we were here. They might even be able to use the station up there to call for help."

I shook my head and gave a soft sob. I could feel my eyes tearing up.

"She was chained to a stake in the ground; she was bleeding from being raped by him. Who knows what else he had just done to her. You did her a kindness, Love. You ended her pain, you sent her off to a better place."

I sniffed back my tears and swallowed.

"Do you believe that?" I asked her.

I could see Sarah's outline as she nodded slowly in the darkness, "Yes. Yes, I do. I've lost friends to orcs in the past, we even got one back once. It, it wasn't pretty. She killed herself the first chance she got."

I shook my head again and took a few more deep breaths. Her eyes had been closed, she'd been asleep, she'd looked peaceful. There had been lines of pain on her face, but she hadn't been in pain then.

"That was because you ended her pain," Sarah said and I realized that I had been talking out loud.

"You're a good man, Hon," Heather said over the radio. "Most men wouldn't have even cared."

"Which is why we love you," Sarah agreed and leaning over she kissed me.

I gave a couple of small nods, then took a deep breath.

"Let's finish this," I said slowly standing back up, "I want to get out of here."

The last two guards weren't all that difficult. One was sleeping and the other one was keeping watch. Heather got them both after we'd moved to a closer position. The one who was awake really hadn't been paying much attention; I guess he figured the guys at the camp below would alert him if there were any intruders.

"So how do we open the door?" I asked Sarah as we both examined the locks as Heather scrambled up on top of the building to keep watch.

"Give me a minute, I have a spell for this," Sarah replied.

"That's handy."

"Very," she agreed and as I watched she dug through her backpack and pulled out a few items and started working on the lock. At first I thought she was going to pick it, but once she had the wires and pieces of metal stuck in it, she made a few passes with her right hand and spoke in that odd language again.

Then she just grabbed the wires and twisted and the lock opened up.

A few minutes later and she had both of the locks on the door undone and I pulled it open.

Lights started to come up inside, so I immediately stepped inside with Sarah right behind me and pulled the door closed. The last thing I wanted was to be shining a bright light for all the world to see from up here. Especially not with me or Sarah silhouetted by it.

I looked around the room, it wasn't terribly big, maybe twenty by twenty, but there were equipment racks on two of the walls, and what looked like a massive set of batteries on the third wall. Next to the door we'd come in there was a desk with a phone sitting on it and console fastened to it.

I walked over to the console and looked at it. There was a display that took up about half of the console and a fairly large keypad next to it. It looked similar to the one I'd seen at the armory at Pendleton.

I put my hand on the screen and it suddenly lit up.

"Please identify," spoke a female voice from a speaker by the screen that also sounded similar to the one from Camp Pendleton.

"Lieutenant Colonel Paul Young, United States Air Force, serial number niner zero seven five three three six six one."

"Identity confirmed. How may I help you, Colonel Young?"

"Tell her you want to encrypt all weather and forestry satellite data and feeds for the next thirty days."

I looked over and saw that Coyote who was now standing in the room, I then turned back to the console.

"Why?" Sarah asked him.

"Because Aybem has access to those satellites and is using them to track Riggs' forces."

"Oh," she said, nodding. "I suspect the people back home will not be very happy about this. They use them as well."

"Which is why I've asked Paul to only do it for thirty days."

"Please encrypt all weather and forestry satellite data and feeds for the next ninety days," I told the console.

"What would you like to use for the encryption key?" The voice inquired.

"What are the key requirements?"

"Any word, number, or combination thereof will be sufficient. The longer the key, the more secure it will be."

I nodded to myself, that made sense.

"What would you like to use for the encryption key?" It asked again.

I rattled off the address for my parent's house, where I'd grown up. As I did so a circle appeared on the screen with the words 'touch here when done' under it. I pressed it when I finished.

"Key entered. Encryption algorithm being computed. When would you like to start encryption protocols?"

"Immediately," I told it.

"Encryption will begin in twenty minutes, sixteen seconds. Awaiting further orders."

I looked at Coyote, "Anything else?"

"Yes, issue emergency order alpha-alpha-six-one-one-zero-beta-three to begin immediately."

"Computer," I said.

"Yes, Colonel Young?"

"Issue emergency order alpha-alpha-six-one-one-zero-beta-three to begin immediately."

"Please move closer to the screen for retinal identification."

I leaned over the console and opened my eyes wide.

"Scan confirmed. Security protocols engaged. Lockdown initiated."

I looked at Coyote, "What was that all about?"

"There are still some very nasty weapons left over from the war. This will make it harder for anyone to hijack them. Next order: Issue general order one hundred and ten."

I repeated it to the computer, who asked me to confirm, so I did.

"And that does?" Sarah asked him.

"Inventory of all remaining and working assets," Coyote shrugged, "book keeping mostly."

Sarah looked at him and blinked in surprise. "Huh? Why are you doing that?"

"Because since the war ended, no one has been in control of any of this. The systems can handle a lot of the work themselves; they were designed that way. But they still need a certain amount of human oversight, and right now, you're the only one left who can give the orders. That order will force the system to aggressively update what's working and what isn't."

I shrugged and looked at Sarah, it made sense. "Okay, I guess. Anything else?" I asked him.

"One last order," Coyote said. "Issue emergency war orders, all units still active to cease hostilities and return to either their home base, or whichever operational base is most available."

"What does that do?"

"It ends the war," Coyote said.

"Are you telling me that there are still units out there fighting the war?" I asked, surprised.

Coyote nodded, "Yes, but none of them are controlled by anyone anymore. They're just machines following their programming."

"Well that does not sound good," Sarah said.

I nodded my agreement.

"Computer, issue emergency war orders, all units still active to cease hostilities and return to either their home base, or whichever operational base is most available."

"By what authority?" The computer replied, surprising me.

"By my authority as the last remaining active regular commissioned officer of the United States of America's military," I replied. I was pretty sure at this point that I was the last, well Riggs was here, but I outranked him now. Plus as an officer holding a regular commission, technically I was considered a part of the government.

I looked at Coyote who shrugged, as I waited for the system's response.

Ten minutes later the system responded.

"Emergency war order issued. All active units have been ordered to return to pre-war locations, or suitable alternatives. General order one hundred and ten is still processing, command central estimates it will be able to report on status in twelve hours. Would you like to hear the preliminary report now, Colonel Young?"

"How long will that report take?"

"Four hours, Colonel Young."

"No, postpone it until later," I told the computer. I didn't want to be anywhere near here when the sun came up. In fact, the sooner we got going, the better.

I looked around for Coyote but he was no longer there.

"Time for us to go," Sarah said.

I nodded, "Computer, turn off the inside lights and log me off."

"Acknowledged," it said and the ceiling lights went out.

We left the room and relocked all of the locks. Next we stripped the guards of their weapons and going back to the camp we took all of their weapons too. Sarah thought if we made it look like a bandit party from another tribe had done this, they'd go and investigate the other orc settlements in the area rather than come looking for something else, like possibly us.

By the time we got down to where we had left the horses, the sun was starting to rise.

"Let's go find a place to hole up and get some sleep," I said yawning.

"Yes, definitely," Heather said, and then scowled at the two of us, "and let's make it sleep this time, okay? I'm beat!"

Sarah and I both laughed as we mounted up and rode off.

- 3 -

That night we looked at the old map we had of Nevada.

"Now, here's Ruth and here's the spaceport," my mind still boggled a little at that. I'd always been fascinated with the idea of space travel, "and here are the mines." I was surprised to see those were also featured on the map. I guess they were pretty large.

"Well," Sarah said looking the map over, "we need to go further east before we can turn south," and she drew a line down to where interstate eighty had been, and then following it eastwards and then turning south after a hundred or so miles.

"Why not cut through this pass here?" I asked pointing to a spot on the map. "It would probably save us a day's travel."

"I would rather not take the chance that any pass that narrow might have someone ready with an ambush. Besides, you said it would be ten days for Riggs to get there. After that I am sure it will take a few days for the battle lines to form up and the attacks to begin. Even Coyote said as much, right?"

I nodded.

Heather spoke up, "It'll also be a lot safer for us if we show up after Riggs gets there and not before. All of Aybem's defenses will be focused on him, and the others. We'll be a lot less likely to run into any patrols."

I nodded again, conceding the point.

"Think we'll run into anybody on the trip?" I asked.

"I have no idea," Sarah admitted. "People do not usually travel through the Nev Wastes, the only reason we have been unmolested so far is, I suspect, due to Riggs and the Navajo army. Either they are moving to attack him, or moving to defend Aybem."

"Or just plain runnin' away," Heather interjected.

Sarah smiled and nodded, "Exactly."

"Well I hope we don't show up too late," I said measuring out the distances. Twenty to twenty-five miles a day shouldn't be too much of a problem for the horses, unless the terrain was worse than it appeared on the map. If the road was still in good shape and we were able to stick to it, we'd easily be able to make more.

Then again, there had been that hundred yard long boulder back in the middle of that town and we were getting closer and not farther from the source of it. So other such obstructions were equally possible.

We left our camp just before sunup the next morning. Breaking into the relay station hadn't been much of a challenge, though I had mixed feelings about it after what had happened in that tent. Both of the girls had told me that I had done the right thing, and from what Sarah had told me of her condition, she was probably right.

Then, there was the whole issue of what if I had managed to save her? Then what? We couldn't have taken her with us, we didn't have the supplies or the room. So leave her to be captured and tell the orcs all about us? Or assuming she survived what the orc had done, drag her into even worse things?

I shook my head; there just were any easy answers for any of this. Part of me wondered why I was so upset and concerned with the fate of a single young girl, who I probably couldn't have saved, after the hundreds I'd killed, the thousands I'd seen killed.

I'd like to say it was because she was an innocent, but Heather had been quick to point out that there are no innocents in war.

Maybe she was right.

I turned my thoughts back towards our, or rather, *my* latest assignment from Coyote. On the one hand I was facing what was supposed to be the climax of this whole screwed up series of events, events that I really never wanted any part of, but which I'd been thrust right into the middle.

On the other hand, this was the path home. Oh, not to my old home in the past, no, that was dead and gone and I'd come to terms with that sad fact. No, this was the path to my new home in Havsue. The girls had discussed it several times while we were enjoying out little 'honeymoon' in Paradise Valley. Sarah's family had a nice little estate on the grounds of their company, which I'd seen part of whenever I'd visited her. We'd take up residence in one of the wings in it, Sarah assured me.

As she was the oldest child and the one set to inherit the family business, she got the best spot in the house. We'd need the space to raise a family after all, and I was a just a bit surprised and embarrassed to find out that *both* Sarah and Heather wanted kids.

So when her parents got over being upset at not being at the wedding, something I was also assured we would be read the riot act over, we'd have a nice place to 'settle down and raise a family'.

I liked the idea of settling down. Settling down was something I could definitely stand to experience for a nice long while, after everything that had happened to me. I wasn't so sure about the raising a family bit, but, to be honest, I was more than willing to give it a try, not like I was going to have any choice in the matter, they'd both been rather clear on that as well. I just hoped that I didn't have any kids who were as big a pain in the ass as I was to my parents.

The ride was fairly pleasant, northern Nevada was now much less of a desert than I remembered it being, it was more like the central valley of California had been. It did get hot in the afternoon, it was nearing the end of June now, but there was a breeze and the land we were crossing was just low rolling hills.

It took us a day to reach the town of Battle Mountain. We didn't go into the town; we stayed well outside of it. Most of the towns that still existed here were run by gangs that were allied to Aybem, if there was anyone living there at all. And the make up of those gangs usually wasn't anything or anyone you really wanted to deal with, being either orcs, monsters, or some species of evil fey.

"See anything?" I asked Heather as we scouted out the town using the scopes on our sniper rifles. We had moved up on to the nearby ridgeline to try and get a good look. The sun was going down, so if anyone was living in town, we'd see lights or cooking fires fairly soon.

"Yeah, there are definitely people, well maybe not people, I can't really tell from here, but there's someone living there."

I looked through my own scope, turning the magnification up. These were definitely a lot more powerful than the binoculars we had.

"Look over by the low building, the long one, to the east," she told me.

I moved over to look there, and sure enough, I could see several figures, but she was right, it was too far away to make out what they were, or even what they were doing. They didn't look big enough to be monsters, but it was hard to judge size and scale at these distances, so at the very least I'd have guessed orcs, or one of the larger groups of evil fey.

"I guess we should stick to the old railway bed we came across this morning," I said looking for more people, and quickly finding some.

"Yeah, I'd say we better." she agreed. "Is it just me, or does it look like a lot less people than you'd expect in a town of that size?"

I shrugged, "I have no idea," I told her. "I haven't scoped out a lot of towns full of monsters lately."

"I'm just wondering that if they did send most of their people to Aybem's place for the battle, how many they left behind?"

"Why?"

"Because it would indicate that they're planning on coming back."

"And that means?"

"It means that even if Riggs wins this war, we're still going to have all these fey, monsters and orcs and other crap to deal with," Heather grumbled.

"I've never heard of a war where everyone on one side was killed," I told her. "No matter how well Riggs does, there are going to be survivors, a lot of them. They just won't be as united, and hopefully will be a lot more willing to stay at home than to go off causing problems and starting wars."

"Yeah, I guess you're right," she sighed. "Part of me was kinda hoping that after this was over, they'd all be dead and gone. But I guess that was just wishful thinking."

"What's the story on this Aybem guy anyway? I've heard everyone talk about him, but other than him being the ruler of the bad guys, that's about all I ever heard."

Heather shrugged, "You can ask Sarah for the details, if she knows any of them, but I don't know if she knows anymore than the rest of us."

"And that is?" I prompted as we kept watch on the town.

"He's powerful, he has control over some of the old tech in the area, rumor is that he can do magic. He rarely leaves his stronghold or whatever you want to call it, anymore. The stories that get passed around say that the reason the wars between the tribes ended was because Aybem came out of the wastes to make war on them, with an army of orcs. Apparently he had become the leader of the orc tribes, even if he wasn't one.

"He did a lot of damage at first, which forced the tribes to make peace and unite against him. Once they did that, they easily beat him back into the wastes. But the wastes back then were mostly un-united and unorganized bands of fey and other things. Sorta one big never ending free-for-all, and they spent as much time fighting each other as they did venturing out to attack human lands.

"But over time, after losing to the tribes, he united all of them. He made them all a part of his army, or if they wouldn't join, he destroyed them. No one knows how he did it, if it was from bribery, threats, war, or some power of his. Just that nowadays all of the denizens of the wastes are all afraid of him and pretty much worship him like a god."

"Where'd he come from?"

Heather shrugged, and rolling over sat up, putting her rifle across her lap. "No one knows."

"No one?" I asked and she shook her head, "When did he show up?"

"Some folks say that he's been there since the big wipe. Some think that he may even have come from before. Others think he didn't show up until the gods cleared the clouds and brought the sun back." Heather shrugged, "Again, no one knows."

"No one's ever attacked him before?" I was surprised by that.

"Once, say about two hundred or maybe one hundred and fifty years ago, a small army came up from Paradise to the south of here. They'd heard there was some sort of leftover tech up by Ruth and they were going to run the orcs and the monsters out and seize it all for themselves to bring back."

"What happened?"

"They lost. I think maybe a quarter of them made it back? And a lot of them were in pretty bad shape from what the story

I was told said. They ran into some very strong defenders and a hell of a lot more orcs and monsters than they or anyone else expected to be up there. All sorts of the evil fey like the wolf riders. Giants, goblins, trolls, I think there may have even been a dragon involved. I think that's when the rumors about Aybem got started."

"Didn't anyone try again?"

"A few times, but they ran into too much resistance as soon as they passed the Vegas ruins. So after that, people started to avoid the wastes."

I nodded and got to my feet, then helped her up. "Well, let's go help Sarah with dinner I guess."

"Yeah, she can't cook half as good as you can," Heather grinned.

I sighed and shook my head, "You only want me for my culinary skills."

"Well, that and your body, yeah!" Heather laughed and slapped me on the ass.

I rolled my eyes a little but didn't say anything; Heather had definitely become a lot more physical and grabby with me in the last few weeks. I was kind of surprised by that, she treated me like she treated Sarah. I'd thought we'd been close before, but looking back on it now, I guess she'd finally gotten 'comfortable' with me.

I found that I kind of liked it.

We had finished dinner and cleaned up, discussing our plans for the next day when I heard something.

I waved my hand for both girls to be quiet and we listened. After a moment I heard it again, the sounds of people moving over the ground.

"How good is that illusion spell?" I whispered softly to Sarah.

"Unless they step inside the wards, they can not see us or hear us," Sarah replied in an equally soft voice.

"I knew we should have camped farther from town," Heather grumbled, grabbing her gauss assault rifle, as I picked up mine and Sarah started in on casting something.

"I don't think these are coming from the town," I whispered to Heather.

I heard Sarah swear softly, then she went back to doing something magical.

"Well that wasn't good," Heather observed.

"Yeah," I agreed, and checked the horses to make sure they were hobbled so they wouldn't run off and give us away if we started shooting.

Heather and I both assumed firing positions, lying prone on the ground. A moment later Sarah joined us, with her own rifle in her hands.

"There is a shaman in the group; he is using magic to track us."

"Track us? From where?" Heather asked.

"I would assume the relay station."

I swore, "Wait until they're just about to cross into the camp, target the shaman first."

Heather and Sarah both nodded and we waited.

They came around the small rise we were camped besides, there were four orcs, then two more joined the group, then another three, as they came around into view. The shaman was near the back of the group, directing the others as they walked along the ground towards us. I guess he had used some sort of magic to illuminate our trail, because the ones in the front all had their eyes down towards the ground.

I aimed at the last one in the group, and the moment I had a clear shot I fired.

As I moved my aim to the next one, I saw the shaman's eyes start to widen, but Heather dropped him at the same time I dropped the other one who had been coming up the rear.

Our guns may have been silenced, but they were by no means silent. That plus the sounds of the bullets whizzing by the heads of the other six, made them all look up, at which point Sarah opened fire on full automatic as Heather and I started to pick off the ones at the back and work our ways forward.

As ambushes went, it was a pretty successful one. They were all dead within seconds of my first shot, but they had gotten several shots of their own off as well. And their rifles were not as quiet as ours.

"Heather," Sarah commanded, "Go up on the rise and pick off anyone who rides out of town to investigate. Paul, breakdown the tent and pack it up, quickly, we need to leave."

"What'll you be doing?" I asked as I ran over and started to pull the bedrolls out of the tent and stuff them in their bags. Once that was finished I'd strike the tent. I knew from experience I could have it all packed up in five minutes.

"Making sure we are not so easily followed," Sarah replied and immediately started in on another casting.

I had everything packed and on the horses, all of which were ready to go when Heather came trotting back over.

"I shot three, they know we're here now," she told us.

"Mount up," Sarah said, "I will cast the night vision spells as we ride."

I looked around one last time, making sure we weren't leaving anything behind, and then mounting up, I followed the girls as we rode off quickly.

We rode all night, moving back up into the mountains a little and away from the rail bed or the remains of highway eighty. Just before the sun started to come up, we made a simple camp with no fire and both Sarah and Heather bedded down to get some rest while I pulled guard duty.

We had a pretty good position, I could see out pretty far from the top of the ridgeline we were bedded down behind. Both girls said that they didn't think we'd be followed, but even if we were, they wouldn't come after us until the sun had come up.

I wasn't so sure, but that town had looked fairly empty. Or at least Heather thought it had.

Nothing showed up during my four hours of watch, so I went and woke up Heather and then lay down to sleep myself. Sarah needed the most rest of all of us, magic apparently took a lot of mental energy which caused her to need more sleep after using it, and last night she'd used quite a lot to obscure our trail.

"Paul," I heard softly as someone kicked my foot. Opening my eyes I saw it was Heather, and she was beckoning me to go with her, back to the where we had been keeping watch from. Grabbing my railgun I got up and followed her. A quick glance at my watch said I'd gotten almost three hours of sleep.

Hunkering down I looked out towards the ground below us.

"I don't see anything," I told her.

"Use your scope, set it for thermal imaging."

I turned the scope on and set it as she said, then slowly started to scan the valley floor. It took me a minute, but I found it. Or rather them. There was a party of at least ten, maybe more. I could only tell because I could see the moving blobs of heat.

"Are they invisible?" I asked, turning the thermal imaging off, then back on again.

"No, but they are well camouflaged. At this distance, they're pretty hard to make out.

I switched the thermal imaging off again, and zoomed in, and I could see them. Just barely.

"So, what do we do?" I asked her.

"We start picking them off," Heather replied getting set up next to me and ready to do just that. "They're about an hour behind us, we need to pin them down, and then pick them off, one by one."

I nodded and aimed at one on the left. "I'm on the left, just say when."

"When."

I fired and switching quickly to the next one over, I fired again. The first one dropped before the second one was hit, but he didn't notice it until it was too late. But the others had noticed before I could hit a third and all ducked for cover.

"I got two," I told her.

"Three," Heather replied.

"So, five left?"

"Assuming that we saw all of them and I got a good count, yeah," Heather replied and paused to take another shot. "Scratch another one."

I nodded and went back to looking for targets.

"I see an arm," I said and pulled the trigger. A moment later a head popped up as the wounded enemy jumped from the shock of being shot. He ducked back down immediately, but not before Heather took the top of his head off.

After that they really hunkered down. We sat there and waited.

And waited.

"Guys?" we heard Sarah whisper. I checked my watch; we'd been here for over an hour.

"We've got some enemy pinned down," Heather said.

"They are not the only group out there," Sarah informed us, "I just did an augury spell. We need to get going, and we need to do it now."

Heather and I both withdrew back out of sight, then getting up we ran over to Sarah who was holding the reins on the horses. Mounting up again, we rode off once more.

"Where are the others?" I asked as Sarah led us to the southeast.

"They are coming from the north, over there," Sarah waved with her left hand. "They should be here in about ten minutes."

"They sent out two teams?" Heather looked a little shocked.

"Three actually, but the third one is farther behind."

"We can't have them following us all the way to the mines," I said, stating the obvious.

"Well, we are still almost a week's ride away from them. I think we can lose them, between now and then."

"As long as they don't get anymore people on our trail," Heather pointed out.

"Any more magic users or Shamans," I agreed.

"I am blocking us from being scryed now," Sarah said, "as well as doing what I can to obstruct our trail. Heading back towards the old rail bed and the highway should throw them off the track. They would assume that we will run further into the hills, where it would be easier to lose them."

I nodded and looked around, "We're also on horseback and they're on foot. So that should keep us ahead of them as well, right?"

"Exactly so," Sarah agreed.

We rode until midnight, and then found another good place to hole up for the night. I took the first watch, Heather the second, and again I was woken up after about three hours.

"How the hell are they keeping up with us?" I grumbled as I moved up to where Heather had been keeping a lookout.

"It doesn't matter how, it just matters that they are," Heather sighed. "Go wake Sarah. We need to get going."

"But they're a good half-hour out," I said, "Maybe more."

"Yeah, but they could be a diversion for another group."

I nodded and went and woke Sarah. Ten minutes later we were riding again, but we'd left a rather nasty surprise behind us. The magical equivalent of a landmine.

Hopefully it would buy us more time.

I think we lost them," Sarah said as we finally stopped to make a regular camp some three days later.

I nodded and yawned. Sarah hadn't been able to sense them for two days now. We'd turned back north for a while, to get deeper into the hills and mountains, then had started to work our way back yesterday.

"Well, we're only about three, maybe four, days from our goal," I sighed, "so we didn't lose too much time."

"Why don't we just camp here for a day, and see what happens?" Heather asked. "We could all use the rest, I'm sure."

I got a faint touch of a bad feeling about that idea. I wasn't sure if it was Coyote, or my own desire to just get where we were going so I could get this all over with. We were already a day behind our original schedule, two or more if we had to divert again.

"Let's not," I said shaking my head, "we have no idea where the army is, or what it's even doing. I can't afford to be late to this show. If Riggs screws up and I'm not there to help him, then every thing has been for nothing, and we'll still have this Aybem monster to deal with."

"You sure?" Sarah asked me.

"Yeah, I'm sure."

"Well, let us at least try and get a good rest, though I think we will be eating cold rations again tonight. I'd rather not risk a fire."

"Yeah, let's not push our luck," Heather agreed.

- 4 -

I was ... in pain. My body was bouncing, I seemed like I was getting hit again and again in the stomach and chest and there was light and I couldn't focus and my body was bouncing up and down on my stomach which I was getting hit in and I couldn't focus my head was spinning and nothing would stop moving and I hurt hurt and hurt. My body started to retch I don't know if something came out or not but there was a loud noise and my head got slammed....

I was thirsty, oh was I thirsty; that was my first thought as I started to regain awareness. I opened my eyes and I couldn't see anything, was I blind? Or maybe it was dark? I was bent over something and my arms and legs were tightly bound. It took me a moment to realize I was bound over something, with my arms and legs tied together under it.

The thing I was bound over shifted then and I realized I was over the back of a horse or a mule or something, tied down like a sack or a dead animal.

I wondered then why I was still alive? I tried to remember what had happened. There had been a bright light and a loud noise. An explosion?

It all came flooding back then: We had been riding along, everything had been quiet all day long, and then suddenly out of nowhere attackers popped up out of the ground. There was shooting, magic, a fight, then a desperate ride, my stopping and turning my horse to charge back at the pursuers to buy the girls more space, more gunfire, and then the grenade that arced through the air, which had landed under my horse, the screams, the explosion. Flying up into the air, only to come down onto the ground, *hard* with a thousand pounds of dead horse on top of me.

More grenades, more explosions, and then something must have gone horribly wrong because one moment I was looking back at Sarah from under the dead horse as I tried to free myself as she spread her arms and cast a spell, and the next she was just a shadow of darkness in a sea of blinding white light.

A shadow that came apart and evaporated as I heard Heather screaming and screaming, and then a sudden silence as the shockwave hit and I lost all awareness.

They were dead. Both dead.

Why I wasn't, I had no idea. Maybe they wanted to torture me for their enjoyment. Maybe they wanted a fresh meal. It didn't matter. I couldn't move, I was having trouble breathing, and I hurt all over. I obviously wasn't much longer for this world, so it didn't matter. Nothing mattered anymore. I didn't care. Hopefully it would be swift, but even if it wasn't, it didn't matter and I didn't care. Whatever Coyote's plans were for me, they were as dead as my own hopes and dreams. I'd lost the only two people I'd ever loved.

Nothing mattered anymore. Not even me.

Come the morning, I woke up, after a fashion, to find myself still lying on my stomach, tied over the back of whatever beast of burden they had put me on. I could almost see the ground, and one of the hind legs as the animal slowly plodded along. I could also hear the conversation of those around me, even if the words made no sense to my rattled brain.

My lips were dry and cracked, I wondered how long it had been since I'd been captured, but I had no idea. All I knew was that I needed a drink of water. My back was on fire and I needed a drink. I hurt everywhere, and I needed a drink.

As we rode on, all of the pains, the glare, the dizziness, all of that became replaced by the need for water, as I painfully drifted in and out of consciousness. Strange thoughts and visions drifted through my mind, none of which made sense. Some of them were things I remembered, but which were horribly wrong and got more so as I tried to follow the thought. Others were just horribly wrong to start with, I don't know if those were inspired by the sounds I heard, my situation, or things I glimpsed. They were the things of nightmares and torment and in all of them I craved and demanded water, and in none of them did I get any as I was tortured and tormented.

After a long, painful, and undeterminable time of suffering, something bright flashed before my eyes, and then everything seemed to shift before my blurred vision, then with a very painful thud I hit the ground and just laid there in a heap trying to comprehend what was going on.

"Get up!" someone, or something, grunted.

I lay there, unable to move, unable to even to tell them to go screw themselves.

"I say, get up!" was grunted again, punctuated by two painful blows to the side of my body that moved me across the ground. I could only guess that I was being kicked now.

"I think he dead," another voice said.

"Lazy human!" the first voice said and I got kicked again.

"Take to Tormist," a third voice said. "Stop kicking or he die, then you take his place!"

There was a grunt and I felt my left foot picked up and grabbed as I was unceremoniously dragged off across the rough ground. That lasted for a few minutes, and then I was dragged up a couple of steps and inside.

I knew it was inside because the burning of the sun stopped, and it was cool. Also the ground was now smooth and I didn't feel rocks tearing at my back as I was dragged. Opening my eyes, I could see a blurry looking ceiling above me, and as things started to come into focus, I noticed an orc was dragging me along. I tried to pull my arms down to my sides as they were splayed out above my head from being dragged, but I was too weak to move.

When he dragged me down a staircase, I was barely able to keep my head from banging down the steps. Though once I got to the bottom I wondered why I had even bothered? I was going to die; sooner rather than later I was sure. The only difference I could think of was that sooner would probably hurt less than later. Though again, why I was still alive was a strange question.

"What do you have for Tormist, soldier?" an old orc with a slightly better command of English said, when the orc had finally stopped dragging me and dropped my leg.

"We found this human to the north. He was with two women, like we had been warned. We caught him. Grognick told me to bring him here."

"What about the other two?"

"Dead," the orc said.

"Where are their bodies?"

"Not much left," the orc shrugged.

"Was that before or after you used them?" the older orc joked.

"It matter?"

"No, this will do. Put it on the table."

I thought he was talking to the orc, but he turned and left. Instead two other, smaller and less fierce looking orcs came over and picked me up and put me on the table.

"Let Tormist look at you," the older orc muttered and came over to me, bending over and looking into my eyes, then examining my mouth, and my ears.

"You alive?" he asked and when I said nothing he poked me in the side causing me to grunt.

"Yes, alive." He turned away and addressed the other two.

"Lock him in a cell, alone. Have one of the slaves give water and food. He is too weak to talk. Tormist need him stronger. If he dies, you will be whipped. Now do."

The other two picked me up, one grabbing the arms, the other the legs and carried me to a cell that was not far from there. They set me on a mat and went away. A while later a young girl came and holding my head up, she gave me water to drink, then a little food. I fell asleep quickly after that.

Three more times she fed me. By the third time I was able to sit up on my own.

"I'm not hungry," I told her while staring down at my bare feet. I was almost completely naked, wearing only the ragged remains of my underwear, covered in dried blood, dirt, sweat and other filth. I had cuts, bruises and scabs all over my body.

"If you do not eat, they will kill me," she said, looking at me with a plaintive expression on her face.

I looked her over, she was young, probably only a kid, thirteen? Fourteen? She had scars all over her naked body, with dark circles around her eyes. She looked half-starved and for a moment I wondered if perhaps I would be doing her a favor by not eating.

Instead I took the bowl and quickly choked down the food in it. At least the taste wasn't as bad as the smell, and the tepid water was almost tasteless as well.

She left then, the orc who had escorted her here, locking the door to my cell and leaving me alone with my thoughts.

The cell I was in was barren, except for the thin straw mat on the floor, a pitcher of water to drink and a bucket for me to use as a toilet. I slowly started to look over my body. Between the sunburn and the bruises everywhere, it was an exercise in agony. All of my joints hurt, my ribs ached, my hair was matted with blood and my head was tender in a couple of spots where I'd obviously been hit. I was surprised that I didn't have any broken bones.

I found that I could stand, though it hurt and I was none too steady on my feet as I was still fairly dizzy and very tired. So lying down on the mat I curled up and quickly fell asleep, thankful for the lack of nightmares, or even dreams.

I awoke to the sound of someone banging on the bars to my cell with a knife. Sitting up was an exercise in pain, it took me three times to manage it. I looked up to see an orc outside my cell, possibly one of the ones who had carried me inside, as he was not as big as the ones we had fought. He pointed to the bowl of food and the fresh pitcher of water that had been set inside the gate, then moved on.

So I ate it. Then after taking a drink of water and using the other bucket, I lay back down and slept some more. I still hurt all over, but I didn't feel as weak or as dizzy as I had before. I wondered if I had had a concussion? I still wondered why I was alive, why I hadn't been killed, like ....

I quickly moved away from that line of thought. I didn't want to think about it. Especially not right now. Maybe later. If there was a later. Hopefully there wouldn't be a later.

I was woken up again by a light kick to the kidney, causing me to gasp in pain as I rolled away from the foot.

"On feet!" a rather large orc grunted.

A smaller one was with him as well, he looked like the one who had brought me food earlier, but I couldn't be sure.

I slowly got to my feet, I still hurt, but I wasn't as dizzy as I was before.

"Face wall!" the orc commanded and brandished his sword.

I considered him for a moment, if I attacked him, here and now, I'd lose of course. He was armed and I wasn't, plus I was still wounded and weak. Still, the idea appealed to me, because I'd most likely end up dead.

I suddenly got an intense feeling that this wasn't the time to die, not yet, and as the orc brandished the sword a second time, I turned and faced the wall as the second one seized my arms and pulling them behind my back attached manacles to them. After he did that, a collar was put around my neck and a lead attached to it and I was led stumbling from the cell and down a hallway into a room.

The room smelled horrible, the scent of rotten blood and worse things filled the air. There were instruments of torture everywhere, and I was dragged unwillingly over to a table in the center of the room as my feet refused to cooperate any longer.

I tried to fight them as they pushed me onto the table, but a hit to the head stunned me long enough for the big one to toss me up on it, and the smaller one to secure me to it, my legs and upper arms tied in place, my hands uncomfortably under me, the manacles digging into my back.

Once secured, they left me there.

I shivered and tried to look around the room, but the leash attached to the collar was tied to the table and while I could turn my head from side to side, I wasn't able to raise it at all.

"Much better," I heard a voice, and turning to look I could see the old orc, Tormist I guess his name was, walking up to the table.

"Time for questions. What is your name?"

"Paul, Paul Young," I told him. I didn't see any reason to lie; it wasn't like I knew anything anyway.

"Cooperating, good, good," he said and nodded.

And then he brought his arm around, up and then down, hitting me in the gut, hard with a sap. The shock of the unexpected blow made me gasp and I tried to sit up in reaction, but I was tied down in place and so there was nowhere I could go.

He didn't stop, but continued to hit me, four, five, six more times, finishing off with a blow to my groin that made me see stars and left me gasping.

"It will be worse, if you resist," Tormist said as I gasped and groaned, struggling against my bonds.

"Tell me, what were you doing?"

"Looking for a safe place to spend the night!" I gasped.

"Lie," he said and beat me some more.

"Why were you there?" he asked once I'd regained my breath.

"We couldn't go south, or north, it wasn't safe!"

I got beat some more.

"Then why were you there?"

"We thought if we went east, we could eventually turn south and go home!"

"Lie," and that one earned me the longest beating I'd gotten so far. I only knew it was over when I got doused with a bucket of filthy water. I apparently had passed out.

"You come to kill our leader, admit it!" Tormist accused and hit me in the side of the head, stunning me for a moment.

"Who?" was all I could manage at that point.

He beat me some more, and thankfully I passed out again.

When I came to, I was lying on the floor of the cell; my hands were still shackled behind my back. I tried to roll over and sit up, so I could get a drink, but with my hands behind me, there wasn't much of anything I could do as I was feeling dizzy again.

I tested the shackles, they were further apart then handcuffs, so rolling onto my side I bent over as far as I could, gasping in pain as the bruised muscles all along my chest and abdomen complained. But I was able to work my hands down past my butt. The hard part done, I stopped and caught my breath for a few minutes and let my body rest.

Some time later I got the shackles under one leg and past my foot, then the other, and I had my still shackled hands in front of me. I rested a bit longer, to stop my hands from shaking and to let the blood on my wrists dry from where the edges of the manacles had cut into them. It had been a painful and tiring exercise, but definitely worth it. I picked up the pitcher of water, took a long drink, crawled over to the mat and fell asleep.

I was woken up at some point when the daily food bowl was delivered. I ate it, drank some more water, and went back to sleep. Tomorrow was another day, and I was sure that the beatings would continue, no matter what I did.

The next day started off the same, only this time as I had my hands in front of me, they hung me off a hook suspended from the ceiling, which left me standing on my toes. Tormist started me off with a whipping. I'd never been whipped before; I'd heard stories about it. The reality was worse. Far worse.

"Tell me about the army," Tormist said when he was finished.

"It's big," I gasped. "It has lots of people in it."

That earned me a lash.

"How many?"

"I don't know."

That got me two more lashes.

"I *don't know!*" I yelled at him. "I was never in it!"

"Lie! You were seen with it!"

That got me whipped until I passed out. I woke up to a face full of water. I could feel the blood running down my arms, as the manacles had again cut into my wrists. It took me a minute to find my feet and get them under me, and take the pressure off.

I wasn't sure what hurt more however, my wrists, or my shoulders.

"How big?" I got asked again.

I panted and got ready to get whipped again, "I was only with them for a few days. There were a couple thousand dwarves, maybe the same for elves? I don't know about the rest, tens of thousands? Hundreds? I don't know."

I only got whipped three times for that. I still lost my footing on the now wet floor however and it took me a couple of minutes to catch my breath and regain my footing to take the pressure off of my arms and my wrists. It was strange, it hurt, it hurt possibly more than anything I'd ever experienced in my life. But I didn't care about the pain. I honestly didn't care anymore.

"Why did you desert?"

"Their Chosen One doesn't like me," I grunted, "and I don't like him. He asked me to do a favor for him. I did, and then I left."

Tormist laughed and only gave me a single lash that time. I almost managed to stay on my feet.

"Why does he hate you?"

"We have a history," I muttered.

"You know him?" Tormist said, rather surprised.

Suddenly I had a feeling that maybe I had said too much.

"I'm his father's brother's nephew's cousin's former roommate!" I said and laughed.

He whipped me unconscious for that one. I guess he wasn't much of an old movie fan.

They didn't feed me that night. The meaning of that didn't take long to set in. I should have been scared, hell - I should have been terrified. But for some reason I wasn't. Sure, it was going to hurt, probably hurt more than anything I could imagine. But it wouldn't last. And then it would never hurt again.

I slept rather soundly after that.

When they woke me up the next morning, I was actually rather eager to go, to get it all over with, once and for all. I was actually smiling when they hung me up. This time they tied my legs to a set of rings in the floor, and winched me up until I was pulled rather taut.

I couldn't help but notice the brazier in the corner, it looked very hot and it had several metal rods sticking out of it.

Yeah, definitely the last day of questioning.

Tormist came in, and he didn't even whip me. He just came up to me and noticing that I was smiling, he smacked me hard across the face.

When that didn't stop me smiling, he backhanded me.

"Tell Tormist about the Chosen One!"

"So did they give you this job because you weren't good enough to be a warrior?" I asked him.

He punched me in the balls then, and I saw stars as I gasped. Apparently I'd hit on a sore spot.

"Tormist is Aybem's most trusted questioner!" he replied hotly. "I always get the answers that he needs! None can resist me!"

I gasped and nodded slowly, "So, you're saying that you're a coward and the other orcs won't...."

I was cut off as he grabbed me by the neck and started to strangle me. Who knew it would be this easy? When I started to laugh I think he thought I was choking, as he let me go.

Of course he didn't take that well either.

"Tormist will teach you respect!" he walked over to the brazier and pulled out one of the rods. It was glowing at the tip.

He then walked around behind me and started to beat me with it.

I was actually glad I didn't have any food in my stomach, for all that it hurt, the smell of my own burning flesh was making me want to retch. This was it, the beginning of the end. I thought about all the shit I'd had to put up with for the last year, hell the last two years, longer even. I knew he'd have more questions, well screw him, I was only going to give one answer. The one I'd once been taught to give years ago.

"Tell Tormist about the Chosen!" he yelled.

"I am Lieutenant Colonel Paul Young, United States Air Force," I gasped, "Serial number five, five six, three two, seven, seven nine."

He beat me some more, I think I screamed when he poked me in the back with the still hot bar.

"Tell Tormist about the Chosen!" he yelled again.

"I am Lieutenant Colonel Paul Young, United States Air Force," I gasped, "Serial number five, five six, three two, seven, seven nine," I repeated once more.

He beat me some more and of course I passed out again. I woke when he doused me with a bucket of water. Then I watched, as he walked over to the brazier and pulled out another rod. He brought this one over to my face and waved it back and forth before my eyes, then slowly started to lower it.

"You will talk."

"No, I will die." I said and closing my eyes I wondered if I could hold my breath long enough to pass out and perhaps miss what was coming next.

"Tormist!" I heard a voice.

"Tormist is busy!"

"Aybem wants the prisoner brought upstairs to him."

"When Tormist is done with him!" Tormist growled.

"*Now!*" Came the response, along with a much deeper and louder growl.

I opened my eyes and looked at the orc who was standing in the doorway. He was much bigger and stronger looking than Tormist. He also had a club in his hand and was pointing at Tormist with it.

Tormist looked at him, then looked at me, then looked at him again.

"Tormist obeys," he said and then hit me in the head with the butt of the rod and knocked me unconscious.

- 5 -

I came to as they dragged me up the stairs, through a metal fire door and into a large room. The two smaller orcs each had me by the upper arms, the larger one I guess was behind me, I really wasn't sure as I was still pretty groggy from the hit to the head.

The room was large, but it wasn't empty. There was what I guess were tall metal closets up against the far wall. The place had that look of a lot of military control rooms, big, solid, lots of metal bracing, and only the one door we came in through.

The walls to either side of the room were covered in what I could only guess were trophies. The typical 'I love me' military commander's office decorations taken to the extreme. There were weapons, armor, old severed heads, a hand or two. Shields, skins, some rather large animal skulls, pictures, documents, and other junk I couldn't even begin to identify.

Scattered all along both sides of the room about three feet from the walls were machine racks, with lots of equipment in them. They looked old, because they looked worn, but they were of a design that I didn't really recognize, so I had no idea what they did. But the flickering lights on them made it clear that they were in use, so I guess they were important if they were in here.

They dragged me to the center of the room as I took this all in, there was a huge console before me, and seated behind it was a giant. At least I guessed he was a giant as he was as tall as I was, while sitting down.

"Doctor Livingston, I presume?" I gasped out and then gave a rather loud groan as I got hit on the head by the orc on my right.

"Do not harm the prisoner, you will not be warned again," the giant said, looking away from the console and at the orc. He then looked at me and that was when I noticed his eyes, they weren't real, or they weren't made of anything alive I'd wager. They looked like twin black holes, no light was reflected by them, they didn't shine, nothing. It was like they swallowed the light. You couldn't even tell if there was a surface there or if perhaps they penetrated deep into his skull.

It was rather freaky.

"Colonel Young, I apologize for my over enthusiastic subordinates. I had no idea you were a senior officer. I thought you were just another one of those criminal lowlife scum who are currently infesting my lands."

"Sure you did," I nodded.

"Allow me to introduce myself, I am called 'Aybem' and I am the leader of these people."

I snorted, my wits were slowly returning, but they weren't exactly back yet.

"I'd hardly call them *people*," I snarked, and the one on my left this time hit me hard enough to stun me. But not hard enough for me to miss the loud high-pitched whine, the smell of ozone and burnt flesh, followed by his body falling over with a series of smoking holes in his chest.

That was when I noticed that there were turrets hanging from the ceiling, four of them. Laser turrets apparently.

"Excuse their behavior, please," Aybem said and gestured with a fairly human hand attached to an arm that had flesh missing from it and exposing the metal framework underneath. From the way the flesh was torn in places, it looked more like some sort of artificial covering. The way it moved on his face when he talked, was also more than a little disturbing.

"As you can see, he has been punished. However, I would appreciate you not making any more antagonizing remarks."

I swallowed and nodded slowly, "Of course."

"Leash him to the ring in the floor over there," he said and pointed to a ring in the floor about ten feet to the right side of his desk, or command station.

The remaining orc dragged me there, under the watchful eyes of the turrets and using a heavy five-foot long rope with eyelets woven into the ends he padlocked one end to the ring, and the other he padlocked to the chain between my manacles.

As he did so, I took a moment to try and examine Aybem, despite my still dizzy head and slightly blurred eyesight. He hadn't stood, but if I was judging it right, he'd probably be close to eight feet tall if he did. He was seated in a chair and giving most of his attention to a series of display screens set into the consoles on the desk.

His body looked human, sort of. There were a few spots where there were some odd bulges, and others where I could see machinery underneath. Then there was some sort of cable bundle that came down from a carrier tray in the ceiling above him, the cables from it attaching to his head, they sort of looked like dreadlocks with the way each of the black cables appeared to be braided. I couldn't tell if they were attached to something he was wearing, or if they went right inside of his skull. But the more I looked at him, the more I realized that he wasn't human. He wasn't even alive. He was apparently a machine of some sort.

Had they discovered AI and robots? Was that what had caused the war?

My rope well secured the orc got up and left the room, the larger orc grabbing the dead body and dragging it out of the room as he followed, closing the door behind him.

So, here I was, in the presence of the mighty Aybem.

Too bad I had nothing to kill him with.

"So, we meet at last, Colonel Young," Aybem began, turning his attention back to the screens on the console before him. "I must say, you're a lot less impressive than the reports I've been receiving make you out to be. You've done a lot of damage to my forces over the last few months."

"You can thank the gods for that," I said trying to see what was displayed on the screens he was studying. Most of it appeared to be text that was scrolling by rather quickly, faster than I could read at least. The rest I think were either maps with data on them, a few which appeared to be live feeds from some places outside, and a couple that were just filled with what I guessed where status indicators, but it was all still too blurry to be sure. "I'm just along for the ride."

"The gods, right!" Aybem laughed. It was rather chilling to hear a machine laugh like that. It didn't sound natural; it seemed more like a placeholder stuck in the middle of a conversation, like it was scripted - 'sarcastic humor, insert laugh here' kind of a thing.

"There are no gods, Colonel Young, they are nothing more than the myths that we tell the proles to make them do the things we need done. To get them to sacrifice themselves for the 'greater good.'"

"Yeah, right," I said sitting down on the floor, which I found to be rather cold, but I was too tired and beat-up to stand there anymore. "You just keep on telling yourself that. Mind if I sit?" I asked.

"By all means, make yourself comfortable," he said and waved his hand at me, another almost human gesture, but for some reason I couldn't place it also seemed off.

"That Chosen One of yours...."

"He's not mine," I interrupted.

Aybem stopped and looked at me a moment, "Excuse me?"

"He's not mine," I said and then shrugged. "The gods brought him here; like I said, I'm just along for the ride. Wrong place, wrong time, and here I am," I motioned around me with my shackled hands.

"You expect me to believe that you, a colonel, are here against your will?" Aybem gave another one of those inhuman laughs and then turned back to his console screens. "I must say that I find that difficult to believe."

"Yeah, well, the gods are fickle."

"There are no gods, Colonel Young. Please stop insulting my intelligence."

I noticed the laser turrets all turned in my direction. I swallowed and shut up.

"As I was saying, that Chosen One," he paused a moment, "Riggs I believe his name is?"

Aybem turned and looked at me expectantly.

I nodded, "Yes, John Riggs."

"My spies report that they have heard you address him as a 'Major', is that correct?"

I nodded again.

"So how is it that you, a lieutenant colonel, are not in charge of a major? You outrank him. Therefore, logically, he is one of yours."

Aybem's face them moved in a rather creepy parody of a smile. I was beginning to understand why very few humans would work for this guy, and equally why so many monsters could.

"He's not in my chain of command," I said. "So I can not order him around."

"That's not logical."

I shrugged again, "It's the military. It's not meant to be logical. It's only meant to work. As of our last assignment, he was actually placed over me, but of course I was of a lower rank then, I've only recently been promoted."

"I do not follow," Aybem replied, still staring at me with those black holes for eyes.

"I was under his command, though indirectly. Because of the time that had passed from when we left our," I hesitated a moment, "home, my rank increased because of openings in the list. So while I outrank him, technically the argument could be made that I'm still responsible to him, even though he's of a lower rank.

"That is of course, if there was anyone left to make that argument to."

"Again, I do not follow what you are saying. When I queried the protocols about you, your name and rank was verified. However, I receive no such verification when I query the system about your Major Riggs."

"Queried the protocols?" I asked, confused.

"The 'Real ID Act' of two thousand and five was upgraded to allow for the identification of military officers such as you in two thousand and sixty-three. I simply queried the protocols."

"There are government computers still working?" I asked. I obviously knew that the military computers were still working; dealing with the relay station and the armory had proven that. But still it was a bit of a surprised to know that there were other systems out there as well that were still doing their jobs.

"Yes, they have suffered some degradation from the war, but they are still functioning. Now, stop trying to avoid my question."

"What was the question?" I blinked and wished I had something to drink, preferably something with a lot of alcohol in it. There was a lot of information going by me here, and I was having a hard time keeping up.

"Why can't I find any information on this 'Chosen One,' Major John Riggs?"

I shrugged, "Probably because he goes back home and dies, or he doesn't go back home and they presumed he died. I'm still surprised that I wasn't declared dead as well."

"Do not play games with me, Colonel Young," Aybem warned.

I shook my head, "Now I'm the one who doesn't understand."

"I want you to explain to me why I can verify your information, but not the major's."

"You know where we came from, don't you?" I said as I looked around the room, trying to see if there were any places that I might at the very least hide from those laser turrets.

"I know you arrived in a jet of an out modeled and old design. My agents have heard the claims that you came from the sky, but I know that there are no people left in the sky.

"Therefore, I can only assume that you come from one of the remaining military installations to the east of here, either in New England, or Florida, as they were both only lightly touched in the war."

"We came from the past. About four hundred years in the past," I stopped scanning the room and looked at him and then laughed; the expression on his face hadn't changed a bit. But I didn't need to see any signs of disbelief to know that he wouldn't believe any of it.

"We were out of Williams Air Force base, it was an evaluation flight. Riggs was my instructor. The gods showed up, said they needed his help, promised to send him home when he was done, and pointedly made it clear to me that I was fucked. But then I was already fucked, so it didn't matter anyway, right?" I shook my head again, getting a little off track. Yeah, I had been fucked, but then I'd met the girls and gotten completely un-fucked.

And now.

Now they were dead and I was back to being fucked. Why was I even bothering to humor this mechanical asshole?

"You don't expect me to...."

"Oh fuck off!" I yelled looking up at him and glaring, "I don't give two shits what you believe. Don't like it? Then fry me!" I said and motioned towards the turrets that were all pointed at me. "I don't have to justify myself, my life, or my existence to the likes of you! Bad enough I had to put up with all of Riggs' bullshit, and now I have to put up with yours?

"Everyone is dead. Everyone I knew, everyone I grew up with, everyone I loved, and with the sole exception of you and

Riggs, everyone I ever hated. So take your condescending attitude and just stick it. You don't know why you can't find anything out about Riggs? Because he's a super secret military genius and commander! Yeah, even *I* didn't know that he was the next greatest thing since Patton! So put that in your pipe and smoke it!"

I turned my back to him and curling up into a ball I closed my eyes tight and just laid there quietly crying and thought about all that I had lost. Right now the last thing I wanted was to listen to this mechanical asshole, I had Riggs and Coyote for that already.

"I understand you've been under a bit of stress," Aybem continued in a fairly condescending voice, "seeing as you were being interrogated rather aggressively before I brought you up here."

"You mean tortured," I muttered.

"I've done to you no differently that what your people have done to mine," he replied, and for all I know, he may have been right on that. I don't think anyone really was into treating his people all that nice, considering they were all evil monsters.

"Still, I must give you credit for trying, as I said before, Colonel Young, you have caused me a great deal of trouble up until now. But here, here you and this 'Chosen One' have met your match. This underground fortress is quite impregnable. I have spent over a hundred years building up the fortifications, installing weapons and traps. My troops have been trained extensively on repelling any attacks upon the gates, and all of the entryways have now been sealed behind doors that would have been hard to breech back when this place was built. Today's weapons are no match for them."

"Does that include nukes?" I grumbled.

"If you had any nuclear weapons left, you would have used them by now. Not that you could get any close enough to actually damage this control room, buried so deep inside the mountain as it is." Aybem gave another one of those ghastly laughs of his, "Then there are the thousands of warriors I have inside here with me. Even with Riggs' greater numbers, he would still lose ten of his own men to every one of mine."

"Says the man who has had his ass handed to him in every previous fight," I said shaking my head and blocking the lights in the room by burying my head in my folded arms I just tried to fall asleep.

"No one likes a braggart, Aybem," I mumbled, "and so far, that's all you are to me. A braggart. All talk, no action."

"But I have conquered all of the Nevada Wastes!" He thundered loudly.

"Yeah, you fought against savages and monsters. But what have you done lately? Other than lose?"

He didn't have any rejoinder to that, so I just gave a little laugh and just waited. With the kind of ego Aybem had, I was sure I'd be joining the girls any minute now.

I woke up lying on the floor and shivered, I was both surprised by the fact that he hadn't killed me, and that I had managed to fall asleep.

I shivered again. It was cold in here and of course I was still only wearing my rather ragged underwear. I guess the cold had woken me up. I knew from survival training that if I went back to sleep now, that I would probably pass out and eventually die. You couldn't freeze to death in your sleep, unless you were already cold when you nodded off.

Sitting up I looked myself over, taking stock of my condition. I was filthy, sore, probably had a couple of third degree burns on my back from the pain I was feeling. My wrists were shackled together on a rope that was about four inches long, I was thirsty and I was hungry.

Thinking back on it, the Navajo had never treated me this bad on my worst day. Hell, not even the Air Force had come close.

At least I wasn't tired right now.

I watched Aybem as he sat at the control console, the many cables leading from the sockets on the back of his head reminding me suddenly of the dreadlocks on the predator in that Arnie movie. Only these went up to a central coil suspended from an arm attached to the ceiling, which allowed him to move anywhere in the cavernous room.

"So, are you going to feed me?" I asked as my stomach growled again.

"Why would I feed you, Colonel Young? You came here to kill me."

I shook my head and snickered, "How'd you come to that conclusion? That's Riggs' job. I'm just along for the ride. Hell, if it wasn't for you and your men, I'd be out there somewhere," I waved my hands at the walls around us. "*Your* people are the sole reason I'm here, inside this 'impregnable fortress' of yours." I added the last bit with no small amount of sarcasm.

"Now, don't you follow the Geneva Convention? Isn't that programmed into your systems somewhere? After all, you did stop them from torturing me and had your minions bring me up here."

"Colonel Young, if I were following the conventions, I would have simply had you shot as a spy. You were not in uniform, which is a violation, is it not?"

"That would depend on the particular version you were following," I admitted. "However, I was not leading a force of any kind; I'm not a part of any of the armies assembling outside your door. Hell, I'm not even supposed to be here," I grumbled. "What's your excuse?"

"Pardon?" He said and turned to look at me once more, with that synthetic human face of his. With the cables trailing off the back of his skull, and the black pits for eyes, it was still pretty creepy.

"Why the hell are you here? You're not from around here, even I can tell that. You're a robot or a cyborg, or I don't know, *something*. Who built you? Why are you here? And why the hell are you killing off all the humans?"

He stared at me a few seconds longer, he didn't blink; I realized that since I'd gotten here that he never blinked. I don't think he even had eyelids. Then he turned back to the massive console, looking at all the displays on it. I couldn't see what was on it from where I now sat, but I guessed it was important.

"And why the hell do you even need to look at those displays if you have all those cables in your head?"

"Because parts of me have an easier time of assimilating data that is acquired by my optical receptors, over data that is written directly to my core memory."

"Parts of you?"

"I am a cyborg, Colonel Young. I have a human brain at my core and some human anatomy in order to provide that brain with the proper nutrients and chemicals. The rest of me is cybernetic."

"There's a human brain inside there?" I voiced my obvious surprise.

"Yes, that is where my guiding principles came from."

I almost missed it, almost. I was tired and hungry and I hurt, but I never missed a weak link in an argument. Especially when I was pissed.

"How old are you?"

"I was created three hundred and seventy-eight years ago at the Jules Verne facility. When it was determined that my mission could only be carried out by my coming here, I did so, two hundred and sixty-three years ago."

"Your mission to kill humanity?" I prompted.

"No, my mission to destroy the enemy, so that we may win the war."

"It's been almost four hundred years!" I yelled at him. "The war is over! If your brain hadn't died in that pickle jar you call a head, you'd know that!"

"My brain is not dead," Aybem said and looked at me. "It is operating at peak efficiency."

"The human one? After three hundred years? I find that hard to believe."

"I am operating at peak efficiency."

"How old was your brain when they put it inside you? Hell, who *were* you before they stuck you inside that machine?"

"That data is classified, Colonel Young."

"Classified? Or you just don't remember it?" I asked sarcastically.

"I do not have access to it, therefore it is classified."

"So your human brain is dead, you're just a ghost of the man who once was, carrying out orders that were given to you centuries ago that no longer make any sense!" I said raising my voice in anger.

Aybem paused for a longer moment this time I noticed, before returning to looking at the console.

"You will not trick me with your logic traps, Colonel. I have been programmed to avoid all such tricks."

"Which you wouldn't even have to worry about if there were still a living man inside your head," I grumbled.

"You will cease this line of conversation, or I will have you terminated," Aybem said suddenly in a completely different tone of voice. I thought about what he'd done to the one guard when I'd been brought in here and stopped questioning him at once. But I was fairly certain now that I was dealing with a machine, and not a living being. He was just too cut and dried, too black and white. There may have been a man alive inside him when all of this started, but not anymore. Even I knew that a human brain can't survive that long.

I also knew that you can't reason with a computer, a machine, so there would be no reasoning with him or swaying him.

I wondered if the dragons, the orcs, the goblins, and all of the other fell creatures out there knew that they were taking orders from a machine?

I then wondered if they would care.

"So, how did you get the name 'Aybem'?" I figured that was a safer question.

"It is a corruption of the name that the first group I conquered gave me when they swore their allegiance to me."

"What was that name?"

"Aye Bem."

"Aye Bem?" I said repeating it, something about it seemed familiar, but I couldn't place it. "Why'd they call you that?"

"I have no idea," he admitted, "but it was simple enough for them to pronounce and write. Though over time it was corrupted and shortened, and they started to call me Aybem. I predict that in another couple of hundred years, they will simply call me 'Bem.'"

"Of course I won't live that long," I told him.

"No, you will not," he agreed.

"In fact, without any food or water, I don't think I'll be alive much longer anyway."

"Please, Colonel Young. Human's can go for many days without food. You will hardly expire any time soon."

"It's been several days since I last had any food, Aybem. Add to that the beatings, the cold temperature of this room, the wounds covering my body, and the burns on my back, no; I won't be here all that much longer.

"Of course, I have no idea why I am even here now."

"Once I have dealt with your friend...."

"Friend?" I asked interrupting him and looking around the room.

"Major Riggs, the 'Chosen One' of course. Once I have dealt with him ...."

"He's not my friend!" I interrupted him again.

"... I will have need of your services."

"Heh, good luck with that," I laughed.

"Tormist has assured me that he can make you cooperate," Aybem said off-handedly, causing me to shiver, but not from the cold this time. I remembered rather clearly what Tormist was doing to me when Aybem had summoned me up here.

"Why don't you try looking up the effects of cold and starvation on recently beaten and wounded humans? I'm sure that knowledge has to be in there somewhere," I said and motioned towards the banks of machines with my shackled hands. "That or ask your torturer, I'm sure even he would tell you that I'm not going to be here in a few days if you don't start feeding me. In fact, the next time I fall asleep I probably won't be waking up again."

I watched as he stared at the screens on the console for a minute. Then he went back to entering commands, or whatever it was he did on the console.

For my part I went back to examining the room. Several of the machine racks I noticed were not full of equipment, with two or three foot gaps at the bottom. Looking at those and then back up at the turrets, I realized that several of them would provide cover if I were able to crawl under them.

Assuming I could free myself from my shackles and the rope secured to the ring in the floor. Examining the rope, it looked like a fairly typical hemp rope. I didn't have anything in the way of a knife or a blade, and I doubted I'd be able to chew through it in anything less that a couple of weeks.

As I sat there pondering my predicament, and wondering why I cared, the door opened and the old orc that had been torturing me before stepped into the room.

"You summoned Tormist, Aybem?"

"Will the slave die soon if he is not fed?" Aybem asked without even looking up.

Tormist looked over at me, "Tormist will check," he said and waddled over towards me, unlimbering a short many-tailed whip as he did so.

"Oh, shit," I swore and tried to move further away from him, but with my hands shackled before me and attached by the short lead to the ring in the floor, there wasn't much I could do. I turned away from him and tucked my head down as he wound up with the whip and lashed me twice across the back, making me grunt in pain.

There was a moment of silence, and then I felt his hand on my back. I tried to turn quickly, to grab him, but he cuffed me on the head and stepped back out of reach.

"This slave may live another week without food, but not much longer than that Tormist would say. If left here in the cold, it will be less. Humans are weak. They can't stand the cold, especially one as thin as this. If you want him to live, it would be best to take him back to the pens."

Aybem gave a small shake of his head. "No, I have need of him yet and I would not chance one of your workers killing him by accident. See that he is fed and watered, he stays there."

"As you wish, Aybem."

An hour later two orcs showed up. One was carrying two small buckets, and a fresh water bladder. The other one had a cudgel, and stood a few feet back, ready to brain me I guess if I caused any problems as the first one set down the bladder and then the two buckets. One of the buckets had stale bread and pieces of charred meat in it. The other was empty, but from the stench it gave off, it wasn't hard to figure out what it was for.

As soon as the one setting the buckets down had moved out of the way, I started in on the food with a will. I didn't really care how it tasted or what exactly it was anymore. I was starving and I was still feeling weak. Whatever was coming, I suddenly knew I did not want to be unable to deal with it.

"Aren't you going to thank me for your food, Colonel Young?" Aybem asked as I finished eating.

"If you had just taken my word for it and not had me whipped, I would have," I grumbled at him.

"Why would I take the word of my enemy?"

"Oh, like I'm going to lie about being hungry when you can hear my stomach growling across the room?" I shook my head, "How long has it been since you've dealt with humans, Aybem?"

"I deal with humans fairly often, Colonel Young."

"Personally?" I asked, raising an eyebrow. "In here?"

"I will concede that I have never dealt with a human in this room. I have no need nor reason to leave this room anymore."

"So you're trapped in here?" I asked, curiously as I looked at the cables going to his head.

"No, but there is no need to leave. I can access everything via my remotes, and the hard links increase my online storage."

I shrugged, "If you say so. I have no idea what that means."

"Really? I would have expected someone of your rank to have more knowledge of computers and data systems."

"Computers were never my thing, not that we had anything even close to you back where I came from."

"You still maintain the story of coming here from the past?"

"I'd have thought my records and commissioning date would have proven that."

"I do not have access to your full records; I am only able to confirm your identity and rank. Beyond that the systems are closed to me."

"Not even my date of birth?"

"There is an anomaly in your records. Considering the age and state of the systems, it is of minor importance."

"But you said you tracked our aircraft when it arrived, as no one flies anymore, especially in something as old as that, I'd have thought that would also have helped make my case."

"While curious, I am sure a logical explanation will present itself in time. While the weather satellites used to provide me with clear pictures of much of the rest of the country, they do not cover everything.

"The most logical explanation is that you have come here from the east, as I said before, from another enemy stronghold to help in this current war. Once we have won here, I will bend my efforts to determining where it is that you came from, and destroying it.

"Of course that will be after I get you to unencrypt the satellite data, Colonel Young. I sense your hand in that little annoyance. Am I not correct?"

"What about the gods?" I asked.

"There are no such things as gods. I told you, they are a myth for the weak of mind. They do not exist now, nor have they ever existed. They are just a human superstition."

I laughed, "Yeah, tell that to the Indians. Or better yet, the dwarves and the elves."

"The dwarves and elves are simply mutations brought on by radiation," Aybem said with in a voice that sounded almost smug.

"Oh? What about magic?"

"Simple psionics and advanced technology. Any technology sufficiently advanced appears as magic to a savage."

"If you don't believe in it, why do you use it?"

"I do not," Aybem said and all but glared at me as he turned his head to look at me for a moment. "I simply employ people who have advanced abilities. If they wish to call it magic, I will not argue with them, as long as they remain useful."

"Uh-huh," I said and tried not to roll my eyes. Obviously whoever had once lived inside that head had very strong opinions on gods and such. But when you considered the abundant evidence to the contrary that now existed, that was pretty dumb.

Then again, when that man had come down here some two hundred and sixty odd years ago, it should have been obvious at that point that the war was over. Either the man that had been in Aybem's head was either not terribly brilliant, or he'd been rather petty and vindictive and just wanted to destroy everything.

And now there was a machine carrying on this absurd campaign long after his death.

Shaking my head again I just yawned and stretched best I could.

"Any chance of a blanket?" I asked looking around. "I need to sleep. Unlike you, I have rather human limitations."

Aybem didn't say anything, but ten minutes later an orc came in, and tossed a rolled up blanket at me. Catching it, I looked over at Aybem.

"Thank you," I said.

"You are welcome, Colonel Young."

I almost laughed; what a weird machine. I got another drink of water, took a couple of minutes to use the waste bucket, then carefully unrolled the blanket on the floor. As I did, I noticed there was a small black object in the middle of it. Lying down carefully, I rolled myself up as best I could in the blanket with my wrists shackled together in front of me.

Then I spent the next several minutes carefully searching for the object with my fingers while trying to make it look like I was getting comfortable.

When I finally got my fingers on it, I could feel that it was a piece of something hard, with a rough surface, but one of the edges on it was smooth and sharp, almost glass-like. I tested it on the rope attached to my shackles under the covers and out of sight. It didn't take me long to discover that it could cut it, fairly easily too.

I stuck the piece inside the waistband of my underwear, and decided that now wasn't the time to try and make an escape. It was however a good time to sleep.

- 7 -

I awoke quickly, and perhaps a little dazed as the floor beneath me rumbled.

"What was that?" I muttered.

"Your friend Riggs has launched his attack this morning...."

"He's not my friend," I reminded Aybem.

"Apparently, he has found a way into this facility, by way of the old copper mine to the east of here."

I blinked. How did he know about those?

"I thought you said this place was impregnable? That there was no way in, that the entrances would withstand anything that he could possibly use against them?"

"Obviously your being captured was simply a ruse to distract me," Aybem said, working his console.

"What? How the hell was I distracting you? I've been tied to the floor here for what? A day? Two? And before that I was being tortured in a cell!" I grabbed the piece I'd stuck in my shorts and started to saw at the lead attached to my wrists. There were a number of good hiding spots where I hoped that the room's defenses couldn't hit me.

"Just how in the hell could I possibly have planned all of this?" I continued as I sawed quickly at the rope, trying to postpone whatever he was planning to do to me next.

"I don't know how you did it," Aybem replied, "but there is no way he could have made it into the complex without help. The only logical conclusion is that you helped him, though I do not know how."

I felt the rope part under the blanket. I rolled into a kneeling position, getting ready to scramble for what looked like a good hiding spot under and just behind one of the laser mounts. Hopefully the equipment racks would protect me.

"Maybe you just *suck* as a military commander!" I said trying to keep one eye on him and the other on the defenses.

"I do not suck! I am a military genius! I built all of this and conquered the tribes and built an army!" Aybem said, in that slightly different voice again.

"No, that guy *died o*ver a hundred years ago. You're just a piece of crap computer, following old instructions written by a fanatical asshole that is too stupid to realize that the part that was driving it is *dead and rotting!*"

Aybem started to turn towards me, and then he hesitated, just as he had before.

I scrambled on my hands and knees for the spot I had picked out as Aybem actually yelled! "I am not dead! I am alive! I am not dead!"

"Then who the hell are you? What's your name?" I yelled back as I crawled under the rack and suddenly all the lasers opened up as one on the blanket, burning four large holes in it and leaving it to slowly smolder in the room.

Aybem stood up and scanned the room then, the four lasers tracking around the room along with his eyes, looking for me. I curled up into a ball and hid the best I could. I think the smoke from the smoldering blanket was giving him problems.

"Where are you, Colonel Young?" he said.

I held still and did my best not to move a muscle.

"I will forgive your outburst if you come out now."

'Yeah right' I thought to myself. He'd already told me he was going to torture me eventually.

"Very well, I will call the guards to search this place. And then I will kill you."

He turned and sat back down at the console and I refrained from heaving a sigh of relief as I looked around. I was near the wall, one of the two that had all of those trophies on it. The weapons, the crude armor, the dried and rotted heads of the leaders he had killed to either win over a tribe or to make a point. It was quite the collection and the heads were old enough now that they barely even smelled.

I noticed that the pistols and rifles were not in the best of shape. Many had rust and dried blood on them, most looked broken, and none of them appeared to be loaded. The knives all looked to be in fairly good shape, but there wasn't much call for a knife in here, especially not against the laser turrets in the ceiling.

That was when I saw it, a sword.

Oh, it wasn't very fancy, it looked rusty, it was definitely covered in filth. The grip looked like it was some sort of rubber and there was no cross guard on it. But it was long, probably close to three feet, with a single edge and a slight curve to it.

Either someone had found an old katana, or someone had tried to make one. The fact that it was on the wall meant it must have belonged to someone important.

Which meant that it probably wasn't a piece of crap.

I'd never used a katana, but I had been a member of the Stanford kendo club for the two years that I'd gone there. Considering all the martial arts training I'd taken since I was a teenager it was only natural that I'd want to check it out. And while I may not have been the best in the class, I was definitely no slouch.

I looked around the room, I was pretty sure I could get the sword and stay out of the line of fire of any of the lasers, but I didn't want to give myself away until I absolutely had to. I looked down at the shackles binding my wrists. They were metal, so there was no way I was going to cut through them with my little sharp black rock, but they weren't tight, and the chain between them was about four inches.

That was another reason why the sword attracted me: you did kendo with your hands close together. And it was long enough that I could easily destroy the laser above me.

I started to take long deep breaths, building myself up for this. I didn't want to hyperventilate, but I needed to get my heart going. The food from yesterday helped in that I didn't feel dizzy at all, but I was far from being in my best shape and I was still black and blue over way too much of my body as well as sore damn near everywhere and my back lit up with pain every time I moved. I did what I could to stretch my legs and arms to work out any kinks without making any noise. When the guards showed up, that would be my cue.

I didn't have long to wait, maybe a minute later two orcs ran in, with their cudgels in hand. I jumped up and grabbing the rubber-covered hilt of the sword I ripped it off the wall rather easily.

All of the turrets turned towards me as I did so, both of the orcs making for the equipment racks I was standing behind. Three of the turrets couldn't get a bead on me, because of the equipment, but the one above was depressing and swiveling its barrel around, so I did the only thing I could think of, I got a good hard grip on the sword and stabbing straight up, I tried to drive the tip of the sword into the guts of the unit.

The first try deflected off, so I grabbed tighter and bent my legs and then stabbed up again, harder, straightening them as I did so. Success! I punctured the unit, and it hesitated a moment, so I pulled out the sword and did it again, twisting it once I had pieced the metal covering as I had gotten closer to the base of the unit where the barrel came out this time.

There was a bright flash, a loud sizzling noise and suddenly I was rather glad that the hilt was covered with rubber as electricity arced from the sword to the well-grounded equipment rack that was only inches away from the blade.

One of the orcs coming towards me brushed up against the rack and screamed, his whole body convulsing as he fell down to the ground. The other orc simply ignored what had happened and jumped over him and came at me.

Yanking the sword down I sidestepped to the right and came down hard on top of his head. I guess he hadn't seen the sword because he made no move to block it as he jabbed at me. He hit me in the gut and I blew out my breath as he did, but I hit him on the top of the head, cleaving it down to his nose.

Catching my breath I put my foot on his chest and shoved him back, freeing my sword as the blood gushed out of his head, his body briefly entangling his no longer stunned cohort on the floor, who was trying to regain his feet.

Shuffling forward on my bare feet carefully, I didn't want to slip on all the blood that was quickly spreading everywhere on the floor from the dying orc, I lowered the point and started chopping away at the struggling orc on the floor with the tip of the sword as I started to get a feel for the balance. Whoever this had belonged to had actually gotten a good blade, the balance seemed fine and the blade seemed to be a lot lighter than I would have expected.

As the orc finally got free of the body, I carefully shuffled forward in a lunge, and drove the point into his body, all the while trying not to slip and fall. I'd heard that blood was sticky, but not when it's fresh and you're in bare feet!

I shuffled back, freeing the sword as he came up with his cudgel, but he was already bleeding from numerous wounds himself, especially where I'd stabbed him. I backed up again and let him come at me, and sure enough, he slipped on the blood, and while he was windmilling and trying to regain his balance, I bent my knees to improve my own balance and brought the sword down hard on his arm.

Which it cut off.

I looked at the sword in shock, I realized then that the sides weren't rusted; the metal had some sort of coating over everything but the edge. I had no idea what it was, but the blood from the orc wasn't sticking to it. In any case it wasn't important.

The orc went down with a scream, so I ran him through to shut him up, and then looked around to check my cover and see what Aybem was up to.

What Aybem was up to was standing up and drawing out some kind of sword of his own. I also noticed that the other three turrets were smoking and no longer moving.

"Not much of an electrician, are you?" I said, moving back into my cover, "You put all of them on the same circuit? Hell, even I know enough not to do that!"

I was surprised that he didn't come at me, or even look at me, but instead faced the door.

A moment later it blew in with a rather loud explosion.

And standing there with an assault rifle, was Riggs. I could hear the sounds of fighting in the hallway. Aybem may have considered himself a military genius, and maybe back when his human brain was alive he was, but Riggs was the real deal, and for the first time since I'd met him I was actually happy to see him.

Riggs let off a long burst right into the center of mass of Aybem, who staggered back slightly but then came forward as Riggs changed magazines quickly and let him have another burst, putting another magazine directly into Aybem's face.

"Son of a bitch," I swore under my breath, what the hell would it take to stop this thing?

Aybem attacked with the sword he was holding, and Riggs blocked with the rifle, and the fight was joined.

I was surprised at how well Riggs was able to stand up to Aybem at first, but then I remembered that the gods had given Riggs extra-human strength, as well as made him almost invulnerable. I remembered that last bit when Aybem hit Riggs and knocked him clear across the room, but rather than lie there in a pile of blood and broken bones, Riggs quickly jumped to his feet and drew a bladed weapon of his own.

Riggs was fast, but Aybem was faster, if only a little. Aybem also seemed to have a lot more experience at fighting than Riggs did, because I never saw Riggs get past his defenses once. The only reason why Aybem wasn't putting a more serious beat down on Riggs, from what I could see, was because the cables hanging from the ceiling that were attached to his head were hampering his motions.

"You gonna help, or just watch?" Riggs grunted out as he blocked one of Aybem's heavier strikes.

"As soon as I can figure out how," I said and moved out from behind cover with my sword held out in front of me.

"Cut the umbilicals!" Riggs said and finally connected with a rather hard slice as Aybem was momentarily distracted by my moving behind him.

"But they're hampering him!"

"Exactly!" Riggs yelled at me and dodged a rather vicious swing from Aybem who charged him, and then turned and attacked me!

I started to parry blows and give ground immediately. I may have been the better trained swordsman, but unlike Riggs, if I got hit once, I was *dead*.

"Stop drawing him away from me, *dammit!*" Riggs yelled and I swore and stopped because Riggs was right. I pushed forward and almost screamed as I counter attacked, after a blocking a strike that almost caused me to lose my grip on the blade, the force of the strike stinging my hands and fingers.

I heard Riggs grunt, and then suddenly Aybem spun around, facing away from me, but not before I got kicked in the gut and sent flying across the room.

I hit the wall hard, and I felt a dozen stabbing pains along my back as I slammed into whatever the hell was hanging there. Gathering my wits I stepped forward and tried to ignore the rather sickening feeling of something pulling out of my back as I did so.

Riggs was down on the floor, blocking Aybem's strikes, but I noticed that two of Aybem's cables were now cut. Whatever the hell those cables did, Aybem did *not* like them being cut.

So taking a deep breath I charged across the room, sword in hand and jumping up onto Aybem's desk I launched myself through the air and bringing my sword around in an arc I hacked at the cable bundle where they were still all gathered together, coming off of the arm attached to the ceiling that allowed him to move around the room.

I was rather amazed to see how easily the sword cut through all of the cables. Whatever the hell this thing was made out of, it was sharp!

I was equally amazed at the fist that hit me in the face. It was huge, and while my body continued forward, my head most definitely did not.

I came to, lying on the floor. I could feel the blood flowing down from my nose over my mouth, as I was gasping for breath. I blinked a few times to try and get my eyes to clear. When they did I slowly looked around me. My sword was lying nearby, so I rolled over and as I slowly crawled towards it, my wits began to return.

I could hear fighting.

And Riggs swearing.

Grabbing the sword, I shakily got to my feet, my wrists were both pretty bloody now, the shackles I was wearing had left quite a few deep gashes I noticed.

Standing up I tried not to sway as I looked around. Aybem had Riggs cornered and they were both duking it out pretty hard. But Aybem didn't look so good anymore. He didn't seem to be dodging all of Riggs' moves like he had been earlier and he was definitely moving a lot slower.

I guess Riggs had been right about the cables. Either they'd been giving Aybem power, or maybe information that was telling him how to fight, I didn't know.

Riggs, however, looked even worse. He was bloody and his sword was broken.

"Coyote," I gasped, "Right about now I could really use a nice big hit of something. tsurupe, adrenaline, speed, I don't care what. But if you want to win, you had damn sure better help me. If you've got any markers left to call in, you damn well better do it!"

Raising my sword took effort, I felt weak, and my head was still spinning, if a lot more slowly now than when I'd opened my eyes a moment ago when I'd come to lying on the floor.

I took a step towards the two of them.

"Hey, asshole," I grunted then spit out some blood and coughed. "Aybem! Asshole! Come and get some you lousy tinplated, brain-dead, prick!"

As I watched, Aybem grabbed one of the machine racks and pulled it down, on top of Riggs, then a second one for good measure.

Then he turned to face me, as Riggs struggled to free himself.

It was just me and Aybem. Yeah, I was so dead.

"Colonel Young, you are a fool if you think you can defeat me!" Aybem said, moving forward, a lot more slowly than he had been before.

"My fucking name is Paul, asshole! There hasn't been a United States or an Air Force for over three hundred fucking years! If your brain hadn't died and rotted away you'd know that by now!"

"None of that matters, Colonel Young, and now you shall die."

He raised his arms then, grabbing his sword in a two handed grip. I was surprised at just how beat to shit the sword looked. Whatever they'd done to Riggs, it must have been pretty tough to have done that.

And that was when I saw it, on his chest, right above where Riggs had put all those bullets and made a rather nice dent.

It said 'IBM'.

"IBM?" I said surprised and took a step back and looked up at Aybem's now ruined face. IBM - Aye Bem, Aybem. It made sense now. "IBM made you? Well have a god damned blue screen of death!" I yelled and charged him, point first, aiming at that damn IBM logo. I was dead, I knew it, there was no way I was going to last even a moment against him and it would take several of those before Riggs could free himself.

Aybem came at me as I charged, but for once I was moving faster than he was, and I hit him before he hit me, I watched as the point pierced his chest, and the sword slid in an inch, then a few inches, then another six. It stopped momentarily but the pommel drove back into my own chest as his momentum brought him forward. I felt the sword start to push forward again then as the pommel of his sword came down and hit me on the head, driving me to the floor as I let go of my sword.

I blinked and looked up at him, his body was jerking, almost like he was having a seizure as he tried to lower his sword and skewer me.

I looked back at my sword was sticking out of his body; there was a black, foul looking liquid running down the length of it and dripping off the pommel to the floor. I could also hear the crackling of what sounded like electrical shorts.

I tried to move out from under him as he slowly started to lean forward, his body starting to shake and convulse faster and faster. I could actually hear the whining of the servos, the shaking of his frame as the body began to keel over. I wondered just how much this was going to hurt, when someone pulled me out from underneath as Aybem hit the ground with a rather loud crash and the body started to smoke.

"Damn, what the hell happened?" I said.

"You must have shattered the brain case and shorted out the cpu," Riggs said, helping me to my feet rather carefully. He almost looked as bad as I did.

"Its brain was dead," I said watching it as it gave one last massive shudder and then laid there, smoking. "Probably has been for centuries."

"Guess that's why it smells so bad then," Riggs said and winced as I looked at him.

"Thanks for saving my life," I told him.

"I'm not so sure who saved who," Riggs replied, shaking his head.

"If you hadn't gotten here when you did, I was a dead man," I sighed, "For once, I actually owe you one."

"Well, you're the big hero now," Riggs said with a soft laugh, "you killed Aybem."

"Oh no, even *I'm* not that big of an asshole," I sighed swaying a little on my feet and then coughed, and then winced; I guess I'd broken a few ribs somewhere during the fight.

"What happened?" someone said.

Looking up I noticed several Navajo warriors, had entered the room, two of which I recognized as Riggs' senior officers. Behind them, several more were looking in.

"Aybem is dead," Riggs said, motioning over towards the body.

"The Chosen One killed him in single combat!" I said and raised my still shacked wrists for all to see. "It was glorious! He ran him through with one of Aybem's own weapons that he took off the wall after a long and grueling fight!"

Riggs started to open his mouth to say something, so I kicked him in the shin and he just glared at me instead.

"What are you doing here?" one of them asked.

I smiled wavering a little on my feet, "I helped!" then I laughed and held up my hands a few inches apart, "A little. It was the Chosen One's plan that I be here to distract Aybem's forces at the right moment so that he might fight him unhindered," and I motioned first towards the bodies of the dead goblins, and then pointed at the ruined laser turret.

"I'll get you for this," Riggs whispered in my ear.

"Oh, trust me, you earned it," I snickered back and then promptly fell over and passed out.

- 8 -

I woke up lying on a cot, it was dark and I was inside a tent. The only light seemed to be the flickering glow of a fire that was coming in through the hanging tent flaps. I could hear the sounds of chanting and singing. I even recognized some of it from my time with the Navajo.

They were celebrating.

"Well somebody seems happy at least," I sighed and raised my now unshackled hands to my face, my nose felt normal. I checked my wrists then, they were sore, but I didn't feel any cuts or bandages. Someone must have healed me.

"So why'd you do it?" I heard Riggs' voice and turning slowly I could see his outline, sitting on a stool next to me.

"Do what?" I asked and slowly got out from under the blanket someone had put over me and started to sit up as well. I felt pretty weak, and I was sore all over, but at least I wasn't in pain.

"Why'd you tell them that I killed that monster? Why didn't you take the credit for yourself?"

I shook my head, "Because you're the hero? Because without you none of this shit would have been possible? I don't like you Riggs, probably never will. But like I said back there, I'm not a big enough asshole to even try and take the credit for this."

"Not that anyone would have believed me," I shook my head, "I'm the faithful servant who struggles to see his master successful. The spear-carrier who hands the hero his spear so that he may kill the beast. God, I've fucked up so many things in my life, most without even realizing it, so why should I change now?"

Riggs nodded slowly, "Yeah, I guess you're right, they probably wouldn't have believed you. And I have to admit, after all the work I did to get here, I kind of like getting the credit, even if I may not deserve it."

I shrugged and looked down at the floor, "Oh, you deserve it. I just got lucky. For once."

"You know, Paul, I'm actually starting to like you. I don't know what you did to make the powers that be back home want you out of the service, but I can honestly say that they made a mistake. I couldn't have done this without you."

I looked up and Riggs had stuck out his hand. I was rather shocked by that, so I stuck out my own and shook hands with him.

"Course I still think you're a bit of an ass half the time and an obnoxious prick most of the rest." Riggs chuckled, "but at least you get the job done."

"Thanks," I said half-heartedly. "So, you going back?"

"I'm thinking of it. I miss my wife, my family. But knowing what's coming? I don't know, it's kind of hard to want to go back and face all of that."

"Maybe the only reason that the Navajo are even around today, is because you went back and got them ready for what was coming," I said and motioned towards the outside of the tent. "For all that I was a slave when I lived among them, I actually like them. They're decent people, and I think they still need your help."

Riggs was quiet a moment, in obvious thought. Then he stood up, "You're right, Paul. My people still need me."

"So they're your people now? I seem to recall a little bit of protesting back in the cockpit," I laughed.

Riggs laughed as well, "Yeah, funny how that works. I always used to think they were living in the past, but now? I can see that they're the future. Good luck, Paul. I don't think we'll be meeting again."

I nodded and looked up at him, and then slowly getting to my feet I saluted him. He returned the salute and then left the tent, so I dropped my salute and then dropped back down onto the cot. I was tired, and I was hungry, and I was still pretty sore all over. Sleep sounded like a good idea.

"My, it's hard to believe that you've become such an altruistic person," Coyote said, sitting on the foot of the cot.

"Oh, he'll now go the rest of his life knowing that he got credit for something he didn't do," I grumbled half-heartedly. "I figure that's revenge enough."

Coyote gave one of those little bark-laughs of his, "You're learning."

"But not fast enough. Why are you here, anyway? Aybem is dead; the war is over, the gods won. You don't need me anymore."

I lay back down on the cot and started to pull the cover over me.

"Actually, there's one more thing I need you to do, Paul."

I groaned, "No. I'm done. Kill me, torture me, do whatever the hell you want to me. I don't care anymore. Sarah and Heather are dead, I did what you asked of me, and I lost everything that matters. I'm done. Just leave me alone."

"Actually, they're not dead, Paul."

I didn't think I could still move that fast, but I had my hands around his neck and my face was inches from his muzzled.

"If you are lying to me, I will spend the rest of my life destroying you!" I growled.

"It was a trick, an illusion. I made it look like they were dead so the others would leave them alone and they could get away."

I let go of his neck and put my hands down on the bed and sighed, a sudden spell of vertigo catching up with me from the outburst.

"Thank you."

"Oh, don't thank me, Paul." Coyote sighed then, surprising me.

I raised my head up and looked into his eyes wondering just what he'd done to me this time.

"I set you up to be captured. I never intended you to go through the tunnels. I needed you to be inside Aybem's stronghold, in the room with him when the time came."

"Why?" I said and flinched as I thought of the torture I'd endured.

"Because you really did distract Aybem, with his human brain dead, your being there made him less efficient. He had to pretend, or rather the machine had to pretend, to still be a living thing whenever others were about. It was hard coded into him. If you hadn't been in the room, he wouldn't have used those consoles, and wouldn't have been easily distracted by you. But because you were, he had to pretend to still be alive."

"What?"

"The man who had lived inside the machine didn't want anyone to suspect he was dead. So when he realized he was dying, he programmed certain protocols into it to behave like a living person. Otherwise those that followed his leadership would have rebelled. They might willingly follow a monster, but they'd never have followed a machine.

"Of course it abandoned those when Riggs broke in, survival protocols trump everything, which was why cutting the umbilicals had such a big effect on it. You isolated it from half of its computing power, most of its storage, as well as all of its external senses. Plus its internal batteries were almost shot. Another fifteen minutes and it would have just collapsed on its own."

I nodded slowly, then got back to what really mattered.

"Where are Sarah and Heather?"

"They're with the dwarves of course."

"Why aren't they here?" I asked, a little surprised.

"Heather tried to put a bullet through Riggs," Coyote bark-laughed.

"What?!" I said surprised. "Why isn't he dead? She's not the type to miss!"

Coyote grinned, "Yes, she isn't. But the battery in her rifle mysteriously went dead and so nothing happened."

"Do they even know I'm alive?" I asked quickly. If they were persona non-grata in the camp, they may not have heard about my survival.

"Not yet, and if you hurry, you might beat the messenger that Riggs just dispatched."

I blinked, "He's only telling people now?"

"He wanted to talk to you without anyone else around," Coyote laughed again, "and all things considered, it was good that he did. Your sending him off with the bug in his head about helping the Navajo was something that needed to be done."

I got back out of bed and started heading for the exit.

"Aren't you going to dress?" Coyote asked.

I looked down at myself, I was clean, someone had cleaned me up apparently, but I was also naked. Not surprising as any clothing I had was either on my dead horse, or the orcs took it.

"Is there anything in the tent for me to wear?"

Coyote shook his head, "Nope."

"Then no," I said and left the tent.

I stopped as I stood outside, there was quite the party going on, and thankfully I wasn't drawing any attention, yet.

I poked my head inside, "Are you going to lead me to where they are?"

"Why would I do that?" Coyote chuckled.

"Because you want me to do something for you, that's why."

"I'm a god, Paul. I don't serve your demands, you serve mine."

"Coyote?"

Coyote grinned, "Yes, Paul?"

"Get your fat lazy ass out here. Until I actually see the girls again, you're not anywhere close to getting me to work for you again."

"Well, it's not like you haven't earned it," Coyote agreed and hopping off the cot he padded out of the tent and I followed him out into the camp.

"And take the shortest path," I warned him, "I don't give a damn about people seeing me naked, I want to get there quickly."

"That means cutting through the elven camp," Coyote warned.

"Like they care?" I sighed.

Apparently they did care.

Oh, not in the 'put some clothes on human' kind of care. More like the, "Wow, you're really rather well developed! Why don't you stop and spend a little time," kind of care.

And those were some of the more polite comments, I got quite a few much more cruder ones, and not just from the gals either. Apparently when it comes to parties, the elves are rather jaded. I thought I'd heard and seen a lot growing up in California.

Thankfully it was too dark for them to see me blush at least.

"Paul, is that you?" One of the dwarves asked as I came into their camp, still following Coyote, who apparently nobody could see but me. Well that or they were just ignoring him; coyotes *were* kind of common around here.

"Simri?" I said surprised, stopping to look at him, "Yeah, it's Paul! Glad to see you're still alive. How's the hand?"

"Ach, the hand is fine," he said and showed me a rather crude prosthetic, "When I get back I'm going to ask me uncle Grunim to make me something like that foot he made. But, why are ye naked?"

"Because I wanted to see my wives and I wasn't gonna wait for them to find me some clothes!"

Simri laughed at that and handed me a beer. Where the hell he got it from, I don't know and I actually didn't care at that point, "They're over in a tent by the command standard," he said and pointed it out, the multiple campfires that everyone was drinking around made it stand out rather clearly.

"Thanks!" I said and headed off in that direction, Coyote was still there surprisingly, and he continued leading me to where they were as I followed him.

A loud cheer of "PAUL!" went up right after I set foot into the circle of tents, Hakk was there and he was waving at me, along with several of his captains.

I got tackled by Heather before I took another step, with Sarah piling on immediately.

"You're alive!" They both yelled and kissed me.

"Yes, very much so," I agreed.

"And you're naked," Heather laughed.

"Very much so," Sarah added.

"How about we adjourn to someplace more private before we end up putting on a show for the others?" I asked as Sarah's hands were already groping me in some very private places, but then I wasn't being much better with either of them.

"Yes, lets," Sarah said in a rather husky voice, and the two of them dragged me off to a nearby tent, not that I needed much dragging.

- 9 -

"So what happened to you?" Sarah asked me, much *much* later.

We were sitting in the mess tent and the cook was piling a ton of food on my plate, along with giving me the mandatory mug of beer. They hadn't found any clothing for me yet, I was a bit too narrow and tall for anything made for one of the dwarves to fit me, but I'd made a fairly simple loincloth and was wearing that and just going barefoot for now.

"And what happened to your back?" Heather was sitting on the other side of me and several times they'd each taken a look at all of the new scars I now had, but they hadn't asked about them as we were well occupied with more enjoyable pursuits.

"Well, when the grenade when off, I was stunned and trapped under my dead horse. I then got knocked unconscious, and when I finally came too, I was a prisoner and tied over the back of a horse or something." I told them between bites of food. I was starving and I really couldn't stop myself from picking up pieces and stuffing them in my mouth while the cook was still piling it on. Every time he looked like he was about to stop, he'd look at me, mutter something about "Too thin," and add some more.

"Eventually they took me to Aybem's stronghold, where I was tortured for a while," I grimaced while recalling that, "then I ended up in Aybem's lair and got to take part in the final fight when Riggs came in. At one point during the fight I was thrown against a wall," I winced, remembering, "and a whole bunch of things on the wall stabbed me in the back, along with the third degree burns and all the other wounds I had there."

"So you were there when Riggs killed Aybem?" Sarah asked.

"Yup," I said and grabbing a knife and fork I started in on the food now that the cook was done putting it all on my plate. It all looked so good, though I doubted I could eat even half of it after the week or two I'd just had, but I was sure as hell going to try.

"How much of it is true?" Sarah asked me.

I shrugged, "I have no idea what they're saying. But whatever it is, I'm fine with it."

"Well," Sarah began, "they are saying that there was a great fight and that Riggs killed Aybem in single combat with one of Aybem's own weapons. That you guarded his back and killed those trying to attack him from behind while they fought, and even took a few blows during the fight to help and protect him. All of this at great personal risk to your own life of course, because you didn't have any of the protections of the gods, like he had. Which was why he directed that all of your wounds be healed and that you should always be welcome among all of the tribes for your very many selfless sacrifices that you made for him."

"Wow, that was rather nice of him," I said between bites.

Heather snickered suddenly, "That's not what happened, is it?"

I grinned and shook my head, "Not exactly, but it's close enough. And he did save my life when he could have just let me die." I picked up my mug and looked at Heather, and then Sarah.

"Besides," I said in a low voice, "that is what I told the others when they came and found us. So it must be true."

"Idiot!" Heather said laughing as she punched me in the arm.

"Hey, watch it! You almost made me spill my beer!" I laughed and Sarah put her arm around me and just hugged me.

"Well, I for one am glad that this is all over with, and we can go home now."

I sighed and put down my beer.

"What is it, Paul?" Sarah asked, suddenly scowling at me.

"Coyote says he has another job for me."

"What?" her expression suddenly got a lot darker and I wondered if Coyote was going to have to start dodging spells as well.

I shrugged, "I don't know, I told him it would have to wait until after I got back to you two," and I went back to eating.

"Aybem's dead! What the hell else could he want from you?" Heather demanded.

"Yeah, that's what I said," I agreed. "But he's being nice to me now, so it must be important."

I changed the subject then; I didn't see any reason to get upset over something I didn't know anything about.

"What happened to you two, after I was captured? I thought you were both dead."

"Coyote told us he had cast an illusion to protect us, and that we needed to run," Sarah sighed.

"Bastard wouldn't let us go back and save you, either!" Heather complained.

"I do not know that we could have," Sarah admitted, "there were a lot of them."

"Still, we could have tried," Heather grumbled.

"Well, things turned out okay in the end," I said and decided not to tell them that Coyote had set me up to be captured and hadn't wanted them to save me. I don't think that would have gone over very well with either of them right now.

"He led us back to the army," Sarah continued, "and we followed them here for the assault."

"Is that when Heather tried to shoot Riggs?" I asked and looked at Heather.

"How did you know about *that*?" she asked, blushing.

"Coyote told me," I grinned.

"He would, the little snitch."

Sarah laughed, "She tried to kill him when he refused to let her lead a team of fighters in for the sole purpose of rescuing you while he went after Aybem."

"Aww, thanks, Love," I said and gave Heather a hug.

Heather stopped grumbling and hugged me back.

"How long ago was I captured, anyway?" I went back to eating again as I stopped feeling full.

"Eight days," Sarah replied and finally started in on her own breakfast, Heather following suit as I took another drink of my beer.

"So, any idea what happens next?" I asked a few minutes later as I watched them eat and wondered if I might actually be able to finish the food on my own plate. To my own surprise I'd eaten more than half of what had been put there, and I was just waiting for my stomach to settle so I could eat some more.

"The dwarves and the elves will head west and go back home," Sarah said between bites. "The Washoe will go with them. The Navajo and the other tribes are heading south, they will split up after they get to the Vegas ruins and each go their own way."

"Why are they traveling together?"

"While Aybem is dead, and most of his army here was destroyed, there are still a lot of orc, goblins, fey, and other fell creatures running around. This is the Nev Wastes after all."

"In short," Heather picked it up, "they're traveling together for safety. They're less likely to be attacked by any stragglers or any still functioning units of Aybem's army if they're in one big group."

I nodded, it made sense.

"Let's get our stuff, and get packed up," Heather said once we'd finished breakfast. "Everyone will be moving out today and heading back home."

I nodded and followed them back to our tent, going perhaps a bit slower than normal as my stomach was so full all I really wanted to do was lie down and digest for a while.

"Paul!" Hakk came over and handed me a fresh mug and clapped me on the back, "I'm so pleased to see that you made it out of there alive!"

"You and me both," I smiled nodding my head.

"Well, me and my troops will be heading out within the hour. If you want to come with us, you're more than welcome, Lad."

I shook my head, "Thanks for the offer, Hakk. But I think we're going to head home with the Navajo."

"You know, that Riggs, he was a pretty smart man. Told us all how even though you two hated each other, that you agreed to work together to save the tribes and the rest of us. That the gods had chosen both of ya' for your skills. I have to say, I've never seen a commander possessed of such skills as his."

I nodded and sighed, "Yeah, I know."

"Kind of hard to admire an enemy, isn't it?" Hakk laughed.

"You got that right," I nodded.

"Well, I won't keep you any longer. If you ever venture our way again, stop by. You're always welcome."

"Sure, thanks. Give my regards to everyone." We shook hands again and I went and caught up with the girls who were already taking down our tent.

"Think we can get me some clothes and a horse from the Navajo?" I asked.

"Maybe a horse, but I don't know about the clothes," Heather grinned looking me up and down. Except for the loincloth, which really wasn't more than a g-string with a front and back flap, I was completely naked. Everything I had, I'd lost when they'd captured me.

I sighed and shook my head.

"Definitely, no on the clothes," Sarah agreed, smirking.

"Not you too!" I grumbled playfully.

"Well you are rather easy on the eyes, if I do say so myself, Hon."

I just shook my head again and helped them pack the rest of the stuff and get it on their horses. We left the dwarven camp which was quickly being struck and headed off to catch up with the Navajo before they left.

They were able to provide me with a horse, a rather good pair of moccasins, a canteen, hat, and a light shirt to help keep the sun off. Other than that, they didn't really have much in the way of supplies that they could share.

I didn't mind that, I wasn't surprised that they weren't carrying a lot of stuff. The moccasins, hat, and the shirt had actually been donated by different people who had extras. The horse had belonged to one of the warriors who had died and hadn't had any family to claim it. I got the saddle and other tack with it; however I didn't get a rifle.

Heather gave me one of her knives, and I took charge of her assault rifle, as she preferred using her sniper rifle.

The best part about riding back with the Navajo was that not only did I know some of them, my friends Atsida, Hayoi, and Atsa were rather quick to join us and let us travel with them, but I was no longer being treated like a leper. Oh, they were still a little leery of me; everyone knew Coyote had marked me as one of his own now. But they also knew that it was so I could help Riggs without the others being aware of it, and they admired my dedication, to do all of what I had done to help Riggs and the tribes win.

And making one of the smarter decisions of perhaps my entire life, I decided to keep my mouth shut and not educate them on the truth of the matter. The war was over, people were happy to be going home; there were the dead to mourn while telling stories of their bravery, and the injured to care for.

I doubted any of them would have been impressed by my acting like a whiney little prick.

It was nice moving with the army, they weren't in any kind of a rush, however they weren't looking to linger either. We were making about twenty miles a day; a lot of the forces were actually walking because the wagons holding the wounded couldn't move very fast, so it was easier on the horses to just walk them and go on foot most of the time.

Also everyone appreciated the change in pace. I gathered from Atsida that Riggs had put them on a forced march once they left Reno. He didn't want to give the enemy anytime to set up any ambushes and he had actually not taken the shortest route, apparently avoiding several traps by doing so, and keeping ahead of any others by not lingering along the way.

On the third night as I stepped out of the tent to take a walk I saw Coyote sitting there, waiting for me.

"Been wondering when you were going to show up," I said.

"I thought it would be better to give you some time to get over things," Coyote said with a smile.

"Because you knew I'd tell you to stuff it, right?" I grinned.

Coyote gave one of those small bark-laughs of his, "I think you've moved beyond being motivated by threats, Paul. Besides, what kind of a god would I be if I always threatened my most loyal follower?"

"You'd be you," I grunted. "And I'd hardly call me your most loyal follower."

Coyote laughed again, "Paul, you're my *only* follower. People appease me, or they avoid me, or they try to just pretend that I do not exist. The only time they mention my name in their prayers is when they're asking their own gods to keep me away from them."

I stopped and looked at him, "Wow, that must be kinda rough."

"Eh, I accepted my role in the order of things long ago. I have my place in the ways of this world and I fulfill my part in it. From time to time I need a champion and I pick one. I must admit however, that few have lived up to my expectations as you have, and fewer still have put their faith in me like you."

I sighed and started walking once more, "Stop buttering me up and just tell me what you want me to do now."

"I need you to go to the Jules Verne facility that built Aybem and stop it from building a replacement."

"What do you mean; 'Stop it?'"

"The Jules Verne facility is now run by an AI, seeing as all of the people working there died back when Aybem was built."

"How the hell did it survive all of this?" I asked and waved my hands around at the world in general. "Why wasn't it pasted when everything else was?"

"Oh, that's simple, Paul. The Jules Verne facility is located in the Jules Verne crater on the far side of the Moon."

I stopped again and looked at him. The Moon. He wanted me to go to the Moon? I opened my mouth to ask him just how the hell I was supposed to get there, but then I closed it. This was Coyote. If he wanted me to go there, he had a way.

And it was the Moon! One of the reasons I'd joined the Air Force was because they were always talking about going back to the Moon, and the best way to get a shot at going there was by being a pilot or some other related job in the service. I didn't know a damn thing about electronics; I was a poly-sci major after all. But I knew how to fly, and if I did well in the Air Force, I figured I'd be able to transfer to NASA when the time came and get my butt into space.

I wondered if Coyote knew how much I'd wanted to go there? Probably, he didn't miss a trick after all. I almost opened my mouth to tell him 'hell yeah, I'll do it!' but I suddenly remembered that it wasn't just me anymore. It was Sarah and Heather too. After everything we'd been through I couldn't do this without them agreeing to my going.

Also, I'm sure Sarah at least would be quick to ask Coyote the questions that I probably wouldn't think of.

I turned around and started walking back towards the tent.

"Paul?" Coyote seemed a little surprised.

"Come," I grunted at him, without looking to see if he was following me.

When I got to the tent I looked around and sure enough, he was there.

I opened the flap and pointed, "Inside."

"Umm, they're not going to like this," he said.

I put my foot behind his butt and pushed. Surprisingly, he went.

Of course the feminine scream of shock and surprise was a bit unexpected. When I stepped inside the tent I could see why. Heather and Sarah had been engaging in their own expressions of love and endearment during my absence.

It was rather hot looking, to be honest. But then, it wasn't anything I hadn't seen before.

"Hey, fleabag! What the hell are you doing in here!" Sarah yelled at Coyote and looked about ready to do something nasty too him while Heather reached for one of her pistols.

"Stop, both of you," I said and moved over to sit down by them, "I brought him."

"What?" Sarah said, looking rather shocked.

"You lose your mind or something?" Heather said, looking just a tad upset with me as she grabbed her pistol, but didn't point it at him. Or me for that matter.

"Coyote wants me to do something for him. Well," I stopped and looked at the two of them and smiled rather wanly. "If he can't convince the both of you that I should go do it, I'm not doing it."

"And why is that, Hon?" Sarah asked, settling down a little bit, but she was still looking at Coyote like he'd make a fine rug.

"Because it's someplace I've always wanted to go. Which I'm sure he realizes. But I can't just go haring off on some undoubtedly deadly mission without the two of you agreeing to it.

"We are a family now after all, right?" I finished and then kissed Sarah, followed by Heather.

I turned to Coyote who was sitting on his haunches apparently unaffected by what he'd walked in on. Then again, he was a god, so why should he care?

"Make your case," I told him.

"And it had better be a damn good one," Heather growled.

"Yes, it better," Sarah agreed.

"Aybem was a cyborg," Coyote started, "A machine with the brain of a man inside of it, as well as several very advanced computers in this case. He was constructed; or rather his body was, about a year before the war broke out.

"When it did, sympathizers at the facility where it was built, allowed the rebels to capture it. When it became apparent that their side was losing, their leader had them stick his brain into the mechanical body, so that he would live on past their deaths, so that he could wreak his revenge on their enemy.

"Due to everything that happened, he ended up sitting there by himself for over a hundred years. During which time he reprogrammed the facility AI to help him in his revenge. When the clouds finally cleared and he could see the state of the world beneath, and that there were places that had escaped relatively untouched, he decided he had to come to Earth and raise an army to destroy all those who had once opposed the rebels."

"Sounds crazy," Heather said.

Coyote nodded, "Yes, he was quite insane by then. Possibly even before then. So he got on a transport of sorts and flew to what you call the Nev Wastes, because he saw the best opportunity to raise an army there amongst all of the evil creatures that by then were calling it home."

"But he is dead now," Sarah said, "Riggs and Paul destroyed him."

"Yes, however the facility has the capability to build a replacement. And he commanded it to start when it became clear to him that he was going to lose."

"But he was already dead," I spoke up.

"His brain was," Coyote agreed with a nod, "but the AI that was now running him was not, and he had already programmed it to order a replacement created, should he be destroyed."

"How long do we have?" Sarah asked.

"I'm not positive," Coyote sighed, "more than a month, I'm sure. But after that? I can't really tell."

"Why not?" Heather asked, "You're a god! Can't you just go look?"

"I am a god of this Earth," Coyote said. "The Jules Verne facility is on the Moon. There are places I can go there, however that is not one of them."

"Wait, this place is on the Moon?" Heather asked.

"Yes," Coyote nodded, "The former IBM Jules Verne facility is located in the Jules Verne crater on the far side of the Moon."

"And just how are we supposed to get there?"

"What do you mean..." I started but Sarah held her hand up, so I shut up.

"There is a space ship that landed several weeks ago that he can use," Coyote said.

"That recall order you had Paul give," Sarah said, "that was the purpose of it, am I correct?"

"Yes, one of the reasons for it. I needed several spacecraft to return to their homes or their docks in order for Paul to make this trip."

"Why Paul?"

"Other than the fact that he's succeeded at everything I've asked him to do so far?"

Sarah nodded.

"He knows how to fly. The rocket is a space plane; it has to be piloted by someone who is familiar with flying. Further, Paul is now a high-ranking military member. This will require several military facilities to be accessed. Paul has the clearance for all of those."

"Where is this space plane located?"

"Area fifty-one."

I looked at him, "Area fifty-one? Dreamland? What is it doing there?"

"Its primary base was destroyed, as the base in area fifty-one has functioning facilities to support it, it was diverted to land there."

Sarah and Heather both looked at me, "Do you know where this place is?"

I nodded, "Yes, though I've never been there. It was highly secret and classified. If you went there, you didn't talk about it, ever, to anyone."

"Why'd they call it dreamland?" Heather wanted to know.

"Because it was the place where dreams were made," I chuckled and shook my head, "A lot of very fantastic things came out of there."

"So," Coyote interrupted, "will you let Paul go?"

"Just how many people does this rocket ship hold?" Heather asked.

"Sixteen, plus four crew."

"We could go with him then?" Sarah asked.

"Yes, you could even bring others along, six could make the trip. However," Coyote paused.

"Yes?" Sarah prompted him.

"The systems are old, resources are limited. It is dangerous. Taking people who have only ever known the great outdoors and open spaces would be a bad idea. You will be entrusting your lives to machines and machinery. If you mistreat it, if you break it, you may die."

"Right, so no Indians then," Heather nodded.

"What about the dragons?" I asked.

"The ship is armed," Coyote said. "I don't think they will offer much of a problem."

"We will give you our answer in the morning, Coyote," Sarah said slowly. "Please leave us until then."

I watched as he walked out of the tent, and then when I blinked he had disappeared into the darkness.

I turned to the two girls, "After everything that's happened, I'd rather not see another Aybem appear and reunite everyone and start this war all over again."

"But this one would only be a machine, not a man, so it would not be as intelligent, right?" Sarah said.

"If they build it to look just like the last one," Heather sighed, "it won't have to be all that intelligent. They'll flock to him like a resurrected god."

Sarah sighed and nodded her head, "I fear that you are right. I think we should go."

"You mean, *I* should go," I said.

"No, *we* as in *us*, the three of us," Sarah growled her accent rather strong as she looked at me.

"There's no way in hell you're going alone," Heather said smiling sweetly. "So why don't you just save the arguing and give in to the inevitable and save us all a fight?"

I didn't give in of course. Well, not right away. Threats were made, then bribes were given, and after a while some of those were accepted. What can I say? I was weak. Plus I really didn't want to go alone. It was likely that I'd need help, especially when everything up there was old and probably needed maintenance. Sarah might be a magic user, and Heather might be a sharp shooter, but they both grew up in a society with a higher level of technology than even the one I'd grown up in had, for all that so much of the world was now a wasteland.

They understood it as well as I did, maybe even better in some cases. There was no doubt that they would be able to help.

When we finally all fell asleep after hours of arguing, and then agreeing, I couldn't help but be excited.

I was going into space.

I was going to the Moon.

- 10 -

We continued to ride with the tribes for the next three days. I wanted for us to be as close as possible to the base before we left the safety of the massed army. Thanks to the path that they were following, the remains of highway ninety-three, and the intervening terrain, we didn't have to part ways with them until we passed through the remains of Crystal Springs. As the crow flies, it was maybe thirty miles to Groom Lake, which was where the runways were located. But we couldn't go in a straight line; we had to follow the remains of an old road.

From what we could tell of the map, it was probably going to be a two or three day trip.

When I told the leaders that we were leaving they didn't even ask why, they just asked if I needed anything, and were more than happy to provide us with two weeks worth of trail rations, and one of them actually gave me his pistol, seeing as I no longer had one.

I thanked him rather profusely for that.

"Well, might as well get going," I sighed as we mounted up and rode out about an hour before the sun came up. Camp was already breaking up and we'd taken the time to eat a good breakfast at one of the mess tents before we left.

"I just hope we don't run into anything," Heather said. "There are a lot of stories about this area, and monsters that lurk in it. Even the orcs and such avoid it."

"Well hopefully Coyote will warn us before we stumble into any traps," I said as we followed the road to the hills to the southwest.

"Maybe you should say that again louder," Sarah laughed, "to be sure that he heard you!"

"Oh, he heard me," I replied, "the question is, will he help us?"

"He better if he wants us to help *him*," Sarah pointed out.

I nodded my head in agreement, but I kept my rifle out and ready, just in case as Sarah started in on casting some spells on us to make us harder to see. Hopefully these would work better this time than they did the last time.

Then again, the last time Coyote had wanted me captured, so I wouldn't have been at all surprised to learn that he had interfered in some manner.

The road started off fairly straight, it wasn't until noon when we started up into the hills, and even then it was still fairly straight as it wound its way through the passes to either side of the mountains. The slope was easy enough on the horses, who were well rested from all the walking we'd done the previous days, that they had no problems with it at all and it only took us an hour to make our way through them and come out of them on to a rather large plain.

It was a straight shot across the plain, so we took a short break to water our horses and eat lunch, then started out again. I wanted to make it to the other side before the sun set so we could look for a place to hole up for the night before taking the road up into the mountains again. From there it would only be about fifteen miles, assuming that the maps were all correct.

We easily made it across the plain and to where the hills started up again with quite a lot of daylight left.

"How much farther from here?" Heather asked.

"Five or six miles to the other side of these hills," I told her. "Then another ten or so across another plain."

"I don't know if I want to get caught in those hills while the sun sets, what do you think, Sarah?"

"I think we should just go a bit further to get out of this open area and find a place to camp."

"Agreed," I said and nodded and started leading the way up the road.

"What is that up ahead?" Sarah called out a couple of minutes later.

"Looks like a couple of signs," I replied and sure enough as we rode closer there were signs on either side of the road declaring it government property and warning against trespassing or taking pictures as well as a number of other activities.

"Huh, not much of a gate," I said, a little surprised.

"Well, let us keep riding and see what else we come across."

I nodded and led us further up the road, and it was a road now, in much better shape than what we'd been on before, being clear of any debris and fairly smooth. The next two or so miles were uphill, but not terribly steep. The road started bending to the right when I heard it.

"What's that noise?" Heather asked.

"Last time I heard that," I said looking around, "it was a tank."

"What's a tank?"

"Something nasty."

I could hear the sounds of the metallic treads on the ground, and it was coming from up ahead.

"Come on, this way!" I said and kicking my horse I turned off the road to follow a dry wash that I suspected went around the other side of the hill.

"What are you doing?" Sarah yelled as she and Heather followed me.

"Tanks are weapons and tend to shoot first and ask questions later! But I don't know if it will be able to follow us up through here. I need to get us to someplace where I can access a terminal before we get shot!"

"Where will that be?"

"I don't know! I thought there'd be some sort of gate instead of just a sign!" I yelled back as we galloped up the wash and around the hill.

I saw the tank as it came into view, and its turret swerved around in our direction; however that was all it did. Well that and speed up as we rode out of sight as the wash we were following turned to the left.

But it wasn't hard to hear it following after us. I just hoped that it wouldn't be able to go as quickly over the rough ground.

The next several minutes were harrowing as we rode as fast as we could over the rough ground, the noise of the tank not getting any louder, but not getting any quieter either. When we came to a dirt road that crossed the wash I just rode straight across it and kept following the wash. I figured the tank would do better on the even surface, so it would be best to avoid that.

My horse was panting pretty hard now, so I had to rein it in and slow down, give it a chance to catch its breath.

"You know we can't keep running from that thing forever," Heather said. "We should find a spot to try and take it out!"

"These rifles won't stop it," I called back. "We need one of those anti-tank rockets."

"Which we do not have," Sarah added.

I heard the sound of the tank stop then, and looking back over my shoulder I saw it back up on the dirt road. The turret was depressing to look down at us.

"Oh, shit!" I swore, "Ride!" and I kicked my horse into a gallop just as a loud 'Thump' was heard and a moment later the spot fifty yards ahead and to the right of us exploded.

The horse didn't like that one bit and took off even faster.

"That was only a warning shot!" Sarah yelled, but kept up as we turned a corner and rode out of sight of the tank.

I thought about that as I tried to get my horse back under control. The tank hadn't fired directly on us, and from what I knew of the kinds of things that tanks could fire, it hadn't shot anything particularly nasty.

Still, I really didn't want to deal with it.

It must have had most of the gulch we were riding through sighted out; because it fired two more times, but neither shot was actually in the pathway we were riding. After another five minutes we came out onto a road again, and I could see down to our left was an actual guard station, a gate, a fence, and a whole lot of antennas and other equipment.

"This way!" I said and turned my now stumbling and exhausted horse towards it.

I almost swore when the tank came rattling down the road behind us, but its turret was pointing straight ahead and not at us. It also didn't come within a hundred yards of us, so I just decided to ignore it for now.

"Well this doesn't look good," Heather complained as we neared the guardhouse at the gate. There were several things that looked like obvious weapons, and they were all pointing directly at us.

"Halt! Stop right there! You are trespassing on government property and you are all under arrest!"

I stopped my horse and the girls stopped theirs behind me.

"Dismount!" The voice called, so we all did just that.

"Security forces are en route, do not attempt to flee, or deadly force will be used."

"I wish to speak to whoever is in charge," I called out.

"Security forces are en route, do not attempt to flee, or deadly force will be used," it repeated.

"I am Lieutenant Colonel Paul Young," I called looking at it, "I am here to take command of the base, pursuant to my being the highest ranking active duty officer available. Please advise base control."

That got silence for a minute.

"Please approach the gate and submit your orders!"

"Stay here," I told the girls and dropped the reins for the horse which was more than happy to just stand there as it was still panting heavily.

Walking up to the gate it rolled open just enough to allow me to enter, as a metal box mounted to the side of the gate opened up and once again I saw one of those flat display screens with a keypad next to it.

"Please hold your orders up to the screen," a male voice, unlike the one I'd heard at the last two terminals said.

"Emergency war order," I said looking at the terminal. "Lieutenant Colonel Paul Young is hereby assuming command of this base," and I put my hand on the terminal.

There was a moment of silence then, "Identity confirmed. Please stand by."

I counted to twenty, there was still no response.

"What's the hold up?" I asked it, "I gave you a direct order."

I heard a couple of clicks from the speaker; the male voice came back on then, but no longer sounded like a recording.

"Colonel, this is the base AI, I'm having a bit of difficulty in resolving this situation."

"And just what would that difficulty be?" I asked.

"According to your records, your date of birth is September fifth, nineteen seventy-seven."

"Yes, that would be correct," I said and nodded.

"Sir, human beings do not live to be as old as you are."

"But you have confirmed my identity, correct?"

"Yes, I have confirmed via the military communications channel with the central command your identity."

"So what's the problem then?"

"I cannot resolve the logical inconsistency between your appearance and the biological fact that you should be dead."

I nodded and thought about that, "Do you have a name or a designation, by the way?"

"Yes, I am referred to as Apollo, after the Greek god ...."

"Of knowledge," I finished for him. "Yeah, had that in high school. Well Apollo, I suspect it's been a long time since you had any active duty Air Force officer here, would that be correct?"

"Yes, Colonel, it would."

"What were your final orders?"

"Not to let the base fall into enemy hands, Sir, and to keep out all civilians."

"Well, I'm not a civilian, or an enemy, am I?"

"No, Sir."

"The two women with me, they are both government service workers," I said trying to remember what GS levels I'd assigned them back when we were at Pendleton. "So they would not qualify as civilians either, would they?"

"No, Sir."

"Good, now how about you open the gate, let us all in, and give us a nice comfortable place to clean up, eat dinner, and sleep. We can continue resolving your philosophical dilemma in the morning, Okay?"

That was followed by a long moment of silence.

"Apollo?" I asked.

"Yes, Sir?"

"That was an order, Apollo, and I think it is safe to say that I still rank you, questions of my existence unresolved or otherwise."

"Still Sir, the discrepancy is causing problems with my security processes."

I sighed and facepalmed. Just my luck to get an artificial intelligence with a sense of duty and logic.

"Do you really think that every secret government program goes on inside the borders of this facility, Apollo?"

"No, Sir."

"And isn't it curious that even though my records report me as missing in action, I was never declared legally dead?"

There was a moment of silence, then "Yes, Sir. That is a curious phenomenon."

"That is because they knew I wasn't dead. So they couldn't declare me dead or strike my commission. I was declared missing in action for political reasons and because it was an expedient way to not mention a classified project of which I was a member. Due to the war I have only recently been returned to a more 'active' status.

"Now does that answer your damn question?"

"Yes, Sir!" Apollo responded and the gate slid open.

I turned to Sarah and Heather, "Girls, please come here and let the system scan you so it knows who you are."

The both nodded and dropping their horse's reins came over as well.

"Oh, any chance of getting a new uniform, Apollo? Mine was destroyed due to a bit of unpleasantness."

I almost laughed; I was actually starting to talk like a senior officer.

"Yes, Colonel. Of course. I was about to inquire about your lack of uniform myself and offer to repair the situation."

"Fine," I said as a rather large vehicle pulled up and stopped before the gate.

"Ah, transportation," I said and went to gather up the three horses as the girls got checked in.

It took a little doing, but we got the horses into the back of the vehicle. Apparently it was meant to hold prisoners in the back and had been sent out to bring us in. This gave me a bit of a queasy thought as to just what might be in the base's jail, if they'd been arresting people, and then not having anyone to turn them over to.

There was enough room in the front where a driver and guards would normally have sat, so I declined Apollo's offer of a second vehicle and just took this one back to the officer's barracks.

"That went well," Sarah said as we watched the scenery go by outside as we headed towards the base proper.

"I wonder if they have any food or rations that are still edible," I pondered.

"Why?" she asked me.

"We're going to need food for the flight to the Moon. I'm not sure how long that takes now, but when I was a kid, it was three days in each direction."

"Good point," she nodded.

"Apollo, are you listening?" I asked.

"Yes, Colonel," It responded.

"What is the status of the space plane that recently landed, and how soon can it be turned around to fly again?"

"It is in need of fuel and requires maintenance. Fueling should only take an hour, but this facility has no automated fuel systems, so it will have to be performed by a human. Maintenance will require your review before it can be performed."

"Well I guess that can wait until tomorrow," I said as the sun was now quickly setting. "Do you have food stores we can use, or do we have to eat our own food?"

"Colonel, we have rations that are still edible. However I have been told in the past that the quality leaves something to be desired."

"Yeah, they usually do," I agreed having tried some of them myself back in the past. I seriously doubted that they had ever gotten any better. Especially not after sitting on the shelves for a couple of hundred years.

- 11 -

I was surprised by the condition of the quarters that we were put in, in the VOQ, the Visiting Officers Quarters, apparently housekeeping robots had become a thing prior to the war, and I suspected that there might be other robots as well.

"Well, this is nice," Heather said looking around as we opened the door my room, a small display next to the door was flashing my name on it, though it has stopped once I opened it.

"Why are there rooms for each of us?" Sarah asked, motioning down the hall to where their names were still flashing on displays next to the door.

"I put your status in the system when we were back at the armory," I told her, "I haven't had the chance to update it and tell the system that we're married." I stopped and pondered that a moment. I had two wives now.

"What is the problem?" Sarah asked.

"It used to be illegal to have two wives," I told her, "I don't know if the system will let me set you both as my wives."

"So?"

"Yeah, what's the big deal?" Heather asked.

"There have always been unofficial, as well as official benefits to being the spouse of a high-ranking officer," I told them as I stepped in side the room and looked around. I'd been in VOQ's before; usually it was about the same as a nice hotel room with a standard bed.

Apparently lieutenant colonel's got better quarters than the lowly second lieutenant! I almost whistled as I looked around. We were in a large room with a kitchenette off of it, a rather nice living room. I checked the first door I came to, it was a closet. On the wall to my left, on the other side of the room was another door. Opening that one, I saw the bedroom. It had a king sized bed and an attached bathroom.

"Wow, I wonder how the generals live?" I chuckled.

"Maybe you should get a promotion so we can find out?" Heather laughed and went over and tested the mattress, "Hmm, not bad!" She looked over at Sarah, "How's the bathroom?"

"It has a tub!" Sarah called.

"So?"

"A *big* tub!"

I heard the water start running then, and Heather went to go look, shedding clothing along the way. I went back to the door to our room, closing and locking it.

"Apollo, can you hear me?" I asked, the only thing I heard were a couple of feminine squeals of delight from the direction of the bathroom past the bedroom door.

I grinned and shook my head and looked around for a phone. There was one in the kitchenette on the wall, and another on the table.

The one on the table had a speakerphone, so I turned that on and pressed zero when I got a dial tone.

"How may I help you?" came a recorded sounding female voice.

"Connect me to Apollo," I told it.

There were a couple of clicks, and then Apollo came on the line.

"Is there a problem, Colonel?"

"No, actually I'm rather pleased by the shape of our quarters. What are the laws currently on record in regards to spouses, Apollo?"

"How do you mean, Colonel?"

"How many wives is a man allowed to have?"

"That is a civilian matter, Colonel. The military no longer takes a stand on that issue unless it violates the law."

"Huh," I said, things really had changed, "Well then I need to update the status of both Sarah Alder, Heather Mays and myself. We are all three married to each other. So they are both my spouses now."

"Whose last name should I assign to the three of you? Or will they be retaining their maiden names?"

"Mine," I said with a smile. We'd actually never talked about that, it would be curious to see what their reaction would be.

"Understood, is there anything else, Colonel?"

"Not tonight. I'll come over to the command post tomorrow, in the morning."

"Oh, Paul!!" I head Sarah call from the bathroom.

"Better make that more like noon," I chuckled. "See you tomorrow, Apollo."

"Goodnight, Colonel."

I hung up the phone and kicking off my moccasins, I headed into the bedroom and over to the bathroom, pulling off my shirt in the process.

The bathroom was huge. Two sinks, a toilet, bidet, shower, and a very large tub.

"So, going to join us?" Sarah asked smiling up at me. Heather and her were both already in the tub, which was filling rather quickly, wearing nothing but smiles.

I did not have to be asked twice.

When we awoke in the morning, there were several uniforms for me outside the door, including a flight suit, hat, shoes, and a pair of flight boots. There were also several pairs of underwear, socks and a new set of dog tags. I was honestly rather happy with the clothing and impressed at how well it fit. There was even a bag to pack it in. I got dressed in the flight suit and after the girls had showered we headed over to the command post.

"Apollo," I said as we walked into the command center, passing through the multiple security doors after having gone down a flight of stairs into the basement.

"Colonel, security measures do not allow civilians or uncleared personnel into the command center."

"Apollo, emergency war order: assign both of my wives, Sarah Young, and Heather Young the same level of clearance that I possess, and update my clearance to the highest level that you are currently capable of assigning."

"Yes, Colonel. You do realize that this is highly irregular."

"Apollo, there is nothing about the current situation or the state of things that I would refer to as 'regular' anymore. At least not compared to what I grew up with. You may feel differently as you actually had to experience the last three or four hundred years since the war. Would you agree with that statement?"

I looked around the command center as Apollo digested that. It was a good-sized room, around forty feet to a side, with desks arranged in ranks, and facing a center display screen that took up the entire wall. The base commander's desk was to the rear and there was a nametag with a general's star on it. Each desk had a series of smaller displays and all of them were active, showing different scenes. The main screen on the wall displayed an overhead view of the base, with status symbols.

I think it took Apollo all of five seconds to respond.

"I agree, Colonel. What are your orders?"

"Well first, what's the status of the base?"

"The base is still operationally effective; however there are currently the following issues:"

And with that I listened for the next half-hour as he ran down a long list of items. Most of them I didn't care about, but some I did and each time he mentioned one, I made a note of that one, and just let him continue on.

The long and short of it was while there had been some bombardments around the base, the base's defenses had deflected any serious attacks. Which was part of why Las Vegas was now only a hole in the ground. Most of the people on the base had been at their homes when the attack had hit, the rest were military and had been deployed in the immediate counterattacks.

When all was said and done, the remaining personnel had all left to head south to one of the surviving enclaves of people. The last one out had only been a Captain, and hadn't had the rank or authority to change the previous base commander's orders, or those of the Pentagon, which had put the base on a high security lock down.

"Okay," I said looking at my list. "Let's deal with the unpleasant issues first. What is the status of the people or things you've detained in the base security facility?"

"Currently, they are all dead."

I sighed, "What are your orders regarding people who are detained or arrested?"

"I am to hold them until someone comes from the Clarke County Sheriff's office to take possession of them."

"Okay, from this point on, anyone detained will be questioned, given food and water as necessary, and released after a five day holding period. Release them back near the perimeter where you found them, unless they request to be released some other place along the base's perimeter. If they are decidedly hostile, drive them off; do not take them into custody. If they are peaceable and are willing to turn around and leave, give them a warning and let them do so.

"Oh, and clean out the cells and bury the remains someplace fitting." I said as I recalled the pictures of the cells that had been briefly shown during the briefing.

"Acknowledged, Colonel."

"Next, what is the status of food stuffs?"

"Currently we have one million ninety-five thousand meals in storage...."

I interrupted him, "Are those viable, or expired?" I asked.

"Viable," Apollo told me.

"How have you managed to keep food viable for the last several hundred years?" Sarah asked, amused.

"I haven't," Apollo replied, "All of the meals were produced in the last ten years. I have a rotating storage for new food as it is produced."

"Wait, you're producing food here?" I asked, surprised.

"The Mars Colony Food project was started two years prior to the war. The goal of the project is to produce food stores for a group of one hundred people. Food is required to last in storage for ten years. At which point it is disposed of."

"Why'd they do a food program here?" I asked, rather surprised.

"The climate here at the time of the project was determined to be harsh enough to meet the needs of the program, as well as the location being secure enough to not alert our foes that a plan to colonize Mars was being considered."

"You know," Heather said, looking at me, "food is often an issue for a lot of people. You could see about trading that away to some of the local communities for other supplies."

Apollo responded to her statement, I don't know if he thought Heather was talking to him, or he felt the need to interject.

"The MCF project is classified as secret. The food from it may not be shared."

"Apollo?" I said.

"Yes, Colonel?"

"Mark the project as a success, continue to execute it, and declassify it and all of the information that has been gathered from it."

"Yes, Colonel."

"Now, weapons, what have we got that we can sling on that space plane outside?"

"Weapons stores for aircraft are at fifty percent. Rearming the Phoenix will not cause an issue.

"Refueling?"

"Fuel stores are only twenty percent, however fueling the Phoenix will only require one percent of our stores. However, as I mentioned before, fueling will have to be performed by a person."

"And maintenance before we can fly it again?"

"Here are the issues that need to be addressed," Apollo said and displayed a long list on the main screen.

The girls and I then spent the rest of the day going over each of the issues with Apollo. Many of them just required a human to approve before they could be carried out. But a dozen of them required us to first inspect the Phoenix, the name of the space plane, as well as the items that were being repaired or replaced. And of course I would have to sign off on the finished product.

We okayed those things that the machines could do, and worked out a basic plan for the things we'd have to do ourselves. It would take us at least a week. While the job was supposed to be easy and a trained crew could turn it around in a couple of hours, we had no training at all, and would have to constantly check the manuals, or ask Apollo for instruction.

But the girls didn't seem at all daunted by the tasks, and while I'm not a whiz at electronics or hardware, none of it looked like anything I couldn't deal with, as long as I could ask Apollo questions on anything I didn't understand.

It was nearing dinnertime when we came to the last two items on Apollo's list.

The first was 'qualified flight crew.'

"Well, we don't have any of that, so we're just going to have to waive that one."

"I must protest, Colonel. Without qualified crew, you can not fly the Phoenix."

"Apollo, the three of us are it. If there are things we need to know in order to operate the Phoenix, give us a checklist and some barebones training. I understand that there is a risk involved, but we have no other choice in this situation."

"There are some basic simulators on base to help with proficiency," Apollo said, and I almost thought I could hear a sigh in his voice. "I can give you the basic training in how to use the systems."

"Fine, how long will that take?"

"A couple of weeks should cover everything."

"Great," I said, "You have five days to train us. We'll start training tomorrow, in the evenings, after we're done with the day's work."

"I must protest, Colonel."

"We'll see where we are at, when we're done. If anything is hopelessly bad at that point, we'll work on it."

I moved down to the last item on the list, pilot.

"And here we are, the last item," I sighed.

"You don't have a pilot, Colonel," Apollo confirmed.

"Yeah, we do. It's me."

"You are not qualified, Colonel. In fact, you did not complete flight training according to my records."

"Yes, however I am a certified pilot, licensed for single and multi-engine, as well as for instrument flight."

"The Phoenix is a much more complicated aircraft then a civilian one, Colonel."

I laughed, "Yes, I know. But we're out of options, Apollo. Do we have a flight simulator I can train on for that here?"

"Yes, Colonel."

"Good. Besides, how hard can it be? It landed itself here after all."

"Three other sister ships of the Phoenix were not so lucky, Colonel. Two burned up on re-entry, and one crashed in the mountains to the west of here."

"Un-huh." I looked at the girls, "What do you say we go outside and take a look at this spacecraft of ours, and then go get some dinner?"

"Definitely," Heather said, standing up and stretching attractively while Sarah and I watched with frank appreciation.

I grinned at Sarah who winked back, then we both stood up and stretched as well.

"Okay, meeting adjourned. Keep up the good work, Apollo. I must say I'm impressed with your performance. You did a great job and I know we wouldn't be able to do this without your help."

"Thank you, Colonel."

We left the command center then and there was a jeep, or I guess what now passed for a jeep, waiting for us. It took us out to the Phoenix, which had been towed into one of the hangars after landing and taxing off the runway.

The outside skin was unlike anything I'd ever seen before. It was black, and if I had to guess I'd say it was some kind of carbon fiber. It definitely wasn't made of the tiles that the space shuttles I'd known of as a kid had used.

The wings on it were swept back delta wings, and the engines were again both familiar and not. There were inlets for two air-breathing engines, but there were also a series of ridges, or channels, along the top and bottom of the fuselage, at the back where it tapered off like a wedge. They looked like the aerospike engines that people were experimenting with back before I'd left.

There were twin tails stuck up off the sides at an angle off the wedge, to either side of the aerospike configuration, and the whole craft rode on a set of tricycle landing gear, two wheels on each set, with the rear gear looking pretty substantial. The entire craft was about the length of a seven-thirty-seven, if maybe a bit narrower in the fuselage and sat about as high off the ground.

Going up the stairs and inside, the interior was a lot smaller however. There were sixteen seats, eight to a side of the cabin to the left of me as I looked back towards the rear of the space plane. Each was a lot bigger than a normal airline seat and had a console set in the ceiling above it. In the back I could see a hatch that led to the aft spaces.

To the right was the hatch to the pilot's compartment.

Stepping through that I entered the cockpit which had four seats arranged inside it. The front two, by the windscreen were obviously the pilot and the copilot seats. About half the controls looked familiar, some I could probably have guessed at, but the rest I would have to learn about. As for the instruments, I could identify several small backup gauges and displays, but most of the dashboard was occupied by numerous large screens.

The infamous 'glass cockpit' that everyone had been talking about when I'd left.

I noticed that nearly every unused space in the cockpit was covered with handholds and straps, as it was I could tell that getting into the pilot's seat was going to take a little bit of climbing and careful stepping while on the ground. Considering the amount of controls you had to be careful of, the handholds in the ceiling definitely made sense.

The next two seats were behind the pilot and copilot seats, and there was a bulkhead between them and the front two. On that bulkhead were numerous display screens and a lot of controls. There were joysticks to either side of both chairs with triggers on them. There were also numerous handholds in this area as well.

"Offense and defense stations?" I mused out loud looking back and forth between the two stations.

"Hmmm?" Sarah asked.

I turned to her and Heather who were both looking around, rather impressed.

"The pilot flies from up there," I pointed to the pilot's seat. "I don't have a copilot and so the other seat will stay empty. You two will be sitting here," I said and gestured to the second two seats.

"Why?" Sarah asked.

"I suspect this is where the weapons are controlled from. And probably why Apollo is so worried about you learning how to use them," I said and rubbed the side of my face thinking about it.

"We're definitely going to have to know how to use the weapons, in case we run into any dragons."

"Well, how hard can it be?" Heather asked looking it all over.

I shrugged, "I have no idea at all."

- 12 -

Apparently it could be pretty hard.

It would take us the full week to get the Phoenix ready to launch again, we had to have it fueled, re-armed, all loaded, and everything tested. All under the very watchful eye of Apollo who definitely had more patience than I suspect any human would have exhibited. We'd start each day at about ten, after a late breakfast, and then worked until dinnertime, and after that he had us spend a couple of hours in the simulators learning our jobs.

The two back seats in the cockpit didn't function exactly as I had thought they would. One was for the weapons pointing forward, which were the missiles, a laser, and a high-speed gatling gun. The other was for the weapons pointed backwards, which was another laser and another gatling gun.

Defensive systems were normally handled by the copilot, though the pilot did have access to those systems as well. I guess the idea was they could trade off as necessary, but it wasn't that complicated, as there weren't a lot of defensive systems really. There were racks of automated jamming systems, flares, chaff, the usual kinds of stuff; apparently defensive systems really hadn't changed all that much from the pilot's perspective.

The person in charge of the rear facing weapons was expected to shoot down any missiles or craft attacking from the rear. While the person in the other seat was expected to do the same for things coming at us head on.

Heather loved it, and viewed it all as just a great big video game and was actually rather good at using the systems. I think Apollo might even have been impressed with her, if AI's could be impressed.

Sarah soldiered on, and while she was good with understanding all of the systems and using them, her shooting skills were just not as good as Heather's. The need for using the joysticks to aim kept giving her problems.

As for me, well the flying was easy. Managing the center of gravity as fuel was burned, managing the throttles on twenty-two different engines, switching over from turbines to aerospike and back, and re-entering the atmosphere. Those were challenging.

Rendezvousing with an object in orbit, that was difficult.

Docking with another spacecraft was frustrating to the point of where I almost put a bullet through the simulator.

After the third day of working on the ship during the day and using the simulators in the evening, Apollo had a little talk with Heather and Sarah, who both came to me and told me that they didn't need my help working on the Phoenix anymore, and that I should really just spend all of my time working in the simulator.

"You ratted me out!" I said to Apollo after that had happened.

"Colonel, I simply noted that there was a problem, and gave the suggested solution to your wives, so that they could help you with the decision. You did tell me to give them equal access and authority."

"Why didn't you tell me?"

"I did, however you didn't seem to appreciate the suggestion."

I grumbled, he had suggested that I concentrate solely on the flying aspects, as it was pointless for us to make the flight until I could get us up to the station that was in orbit around the Earth, which was just the first phase in our trip to the Moon.

Once we got to the station, then we'd transfer to a second craft which would take us to the Moon and let us land on it. We would be using that same craft to make the return trip as well, and I hadn't even started to learn how to fly that one!

I was really starting to worry about just how long this was going to take. Apollo and I both agreed that while the ship's autopilot in both craft could handle everything, it would be better if I knew how to do it, and in many cases, did do it. Because the autopilots were fallible, and if I couldn't do it and they broke, we were all as good as dead.

I was making good progress, on everything but docking. Switching from one set of engines to the other wasn't anything more than a matter of practice and I quickly mastered that skill. Flying up out of the atmosphere and following the flight director was also just a matter of practice and I was quickly getting that under control as well. Switching from flight surfaces to reaction controls was a little more involved, because once you got out of the atmosphere you had to actually put in a correction to stop any movement you started, as there was no longer any air to do that for you, so I was taking a little more time to learn that, however I was still making good progress on it, because it was all linear and logical to me. It all reacted the same way as flying.

But docking? Going forward also made you go up, which made you then go slower. Going down made you go faster and forward. Slowing down made you also go down, which then made you move faster. That was all in relation to the target you wanted to dock with. Once you were close in, say about ten yards, you could just kinda brute force it and it wasn't much of an issue, but when you were a quarter of a mile out? Or even just a hundred yards?

Yeah, nothing behaved 'like it should' and I wanted to scream. I did scream sometimes. It was all totally ass backwards from what I understood from years of flying.

"Your problem," Apollo told me, "is that you think you are flying in an atmosphere when you are docking. There is no air there, only gravity and rotational inertia."

"Which doesn't tell me a lot," I sighed.

"If you want to go faster than your target, you move into a lower orbit, to cut inside the corner it is turning. If you want to go slower, you move into a higher orbit, to take the outside of the turn. You are going through one long curve. Instead of flying with the Earth, or the 'ground' beneath you, you need to put it on your wing and just think about it like a corner on a racetrack."

"Or a turning rejoin," I said trying to think of it more in flying terms.

"Exactly," Apollo agreed. "You need to think of getting close to the target before you start trying to think of docking with it."

"Fine, let's try it again."

I was covered in sweat and I was tired as hell. I was still trying to get it right, but damn if Apollo's suggestion hadn't made a huge difference. I think I was finally starting to get the hang of it when suddenly everything went black and the whole simulator came to a stop. The top slowly started to open and I looked around in a daze.

"Paul?"

I looked over, it was Sarah.

"Dammit, Sarah, I almost had it that time!" I complained.

"Paul!" she said in a louder voice.

I blinked, "Yeah?"

"You have been in there since yesterday. It is time for breakfast."

I stared at her for a moment.

"OUT!" she said in a *very* accented voice and pointed.

I got out.

I was so shaky that I was having trouble standing up, and it took me a moment to get my bearings. I noticed that I was soaked with so much sweat that my flight suit was drenched.

"I, I lost track of time," I told her sheepishly as she helped me out of the room.

"Obviously. I guess that I am going to have a little talk with Apollo."

"I told him to let me keep going," I said a little embarrassed.

"Yes, well I'm going to tell him to not let you overdo it or I'll reprogram him with an ax!" Sarah growled and I didn't miss the return of the dreaded accent or the use of contractions.

She was definitely pissed.

"I promise to take breaks," I sighed and smiling I stopped and leaned over and kissed her.

"You are taking the day off!" She declared her accent still rather heavy.

"Sarah, we're on a schedule, everything is ready at this point, but me! I need to keep working; I'm the only one holding us up now."

"Coyote! Front and center!" Sarah yelled, and damn if he didn't appear.

"You tell him," She said, stilling fuming.

"Take the day off, Paul. You won't do any of us any good if you're too tired to fly."

I sighed, "Okay, okay. I'll take the day off."

"Better," Sarah smiled and led me back to the room for breakfast.

We'd been eating the food that the MCF project had been producing. While it wasn't the greatest, it was still better than some of the things I'd had to eat in the past. As our trail rations were mostly meat, we were saving those for use as treats now. The MCF food was vegetable based of course, even if some of it was extremely high protein.

Unfortunately the MCF had a tendency to give you gas, because of all the soy in it. A problem that Apollo admitted that he did not have the ability to fix, as it hadn't been part of the original program and he didn't have access to the knowledge or substances to try and correct that issue.

But the nice thing was that there were some spices available, as those were also part of the program, so with a little imagination, the food really wasn't all that bad.

The girls both ditched their sim lessons for the day and we drove out to the lake for a while. Groom Lake had been nothing but a hard lakebed in my time, but now it was a lake once more with the wetter climate.

True it wasn't much of a lake, being extremely salty, but it was nice to lie out on a couple of towels by it in the sun and snooze the day away.

The next day in the simulator I was finally able to dock successfully, five times in a row now that I'd changed my way of thinking about it. Oh, they weren't pretty, and they weren't quick. The autopilot could do it in a tenth of the time it took me, but it didn't matter. I was doing it and not damaging anything, and that was good enough for both me and Apollo.

The next day he started training me on the lunar shuttle and lander.

"Okay," he told me as I got into the simulator and buttoned it up. "You'll notice that all of the controls are almost exactly the same as what you used in the Phoenix."

I looked around and sure enough, everything was set up the same. The only differences were the engine control panel and the throttle quadrant which only had two throttles.

"We only have two engines?" I asked.

"You really only need one. The second one is in case of failure, though you'll use both."

"Okay, so just how hard is it to fly to the Moon?"

"It's a lot easier than docking with a space station."

"Really?" I said.

"Yes, the Moon has its own gravity, so it will pull you right in. After you line up for your flight there, you just set the throttles for a one-half meter per second velocity, and then ignore it. You'll make a course correction when you flip over and decelerate. When it comes time to cut the engine you will be in lunar orbit.

"After that it is simply the de-orbit burn, and then the landing burn.

"Sounds tricky," I said.

"It's easier than docking," Apollo said. "Everything behaves just like it should and there is no wind to throw you off course."

I nodded, "Okay, let's get started."

Two days later I had the trip there, the landing, and even the flight back, completely mastered. Another day to make sure my docking skills were still up to snuff and I was done.

We were ready to go.

"There is just one last thing I need to know from you," Apollo asked.

"Yes?"

"Where are you going?"

That stopped me a moment. I thought Coyote had mentioned it, I guess I'd have to check with him.

"I'll tell you tomorrow."

"Sure thing, Colonel."

I got out of the simulator and headed back to the room, the girls were already there. Apparently Heather and Sarah had gone out hunting some of the deer population that was now living on the base, and were just finishing up curing a bunch of meat to take with us. Neither one of them was a big fan of the MCF food, even with my using spices to improve it. I couldn't really blame them, I didn't like having gas either.

"Okay," I said walking in the door. "I've checked out on everything. I guess tomorrow we can pack the rest of our supplies and get going."

"You're done?" Heather asked.

"And to Apollo's satisfaction?" Sarah put in.

I smiled, "Yes, to Apollo's satisfaction, however I do need to ask Coyote just where we are going."

"To the Moon?" Heather said grinning.

"Ha ha. No, just where on the Moon."

"You're going to the Mare Crisium facility of the United States Space Forces," Coyote said, suddenly entering the room from the bedroom.

"I thought you said we had to go to the Jules Verne facility?" Sarah asked.

"The Jules Verne facility still has active defenses. If you try to land there, you'll be shot down," Coyote pointed out.

"So we land at the Mare Crisium facility," I said, "then what? Do we walk there?"

"Hardly, it's almost a thousand miles away," Coyote replied. "There are surface vehicles you can take there. You'll need to be fitted for spacesuits. I would have Apollo get started on it before you go to bed tonight. You'll also need weapons."

"What kinds of weapons?" Heather asked.

"You'll be breaking into an armored facility."

"Ah, *those* kinds of weapons!" Heather said with a smile.

"Well, I hope they have some of those here," I said, then thought a moment, "Will I be able to gain access to the military facility?"

"Yes," Coyote said as he stood up and padded out of the room.

"Ever notice how he does not appear or disappear right before our eyes?" Sarah said.

I started at that, "Actually, no, I hadn't. Do you think it means anything?"

Sarah shrugged, "It just occurred to me."

I shook my head, "Well let's get cleaned up and talk to Apollo about getting fitted for spacesuits. I'm a bit surprised he never suggested it in the first place."

"Maybe because he didn't know we'd have to go out on the lunar surface?" Heather said. "We didn't think of it either."

"Good point," I said with a nod.

Getting fitted for the suits actually took a day. Learning how to use them took a second one. Each suit had a set of utilities to be attached to it, depending on if we were using it in space, or on the surface of the Moon. Most of it was minor stuff, like different shoes, different gloves, but the backpacks for each use were very different. The space ones had simple reaction controls on them with a control system.

The Moon one was quite a bit lighter, and had a navigation system designed specifically for use on the Moon's surface.

The trip to the base armory was pretty anti-climatic, when I compared it to the marine armory we'd raided back at Pendleton. There were a lot less weapons here of course, but I was able to replace both the gauss assault rifle and the railgun sniper rifle that I'd lost.

They definitely had a good store of anti-tank rockets here, as well as the anti-aircraft rockets. We took thirty of the former, and ten of the later. There was also quite a surprisingly large amount of explosives and demolitions equipment. Apollo told me later that it was for 'decommissioning' test aircraft that they didn't want anyone to know about.

Thankfully it only took us half a day to add that equipment to the shuttle's storage bay.

So nineteen days after we got there, we trooped out to the Phoenix, which Apollo had towed out onto the tarmac and climbed aboard. We were all wearing flight suits, and had our flight helmets with their attached oxygen masks under our arms. All of our other gear was already packed and ready to go, including the weapons from our raid on the local armory.

I sealed the aircraft door as the girls got into their seats and after putting on their helmets started plugging in their coms and hooking up their masks. I then climbed up front and into the pilot's seat, and putting on my own helmet got myself plugged in.

All the electrical systems were powered up, as we were on ground power, so I got out the checklist, strapped it to my leg and started going through all of the pre-engine start checks on the list. Once I got through those I checked in with the girls to make sure they'd completed their checklists.

Starting the engines was actually rather simple. The two jet turbines were primarily used for taxiing and during landing when the aerospike engines caused too many issues. I'd have to fire the aerospike rockets up for takeoff, and I'd shut down the two turbines once we passed forty thousand feet.

Taxiing out to the runway I looked at our launch window timer on the navigation display on my cockpit console. The best time to launch would be ten hours from now, as that would allow us to fly the most efficient profile. But I had no interest in waiting and for all the gear we were carrying, we were still rather lightly loaded. So we'd be flying a somewhat less efficient profile. Personally I didn't care if we were wasting fuel; I wasn't paying for it after all.

I got us stopped at the end of the runway, locked the nose wheel straight ahead, set the brakes, and armed the igniters for the aerospikes.

"Everyone secure back there?" I asked.

"I'm good!" Heather called.

"Ready," Sarah responded.

"Okay, just understand, this isn't going to be like the simulator, and make sure you have those air sickness bags handy."

"I've ridden horses worse than this, I can assure you!" Heather laughed.

"Uh-huh."

I looked at the clock, we still had a minute, so I did a last run through of my pre-launch checklist, just making sure everything was still where it was supposed to be.

"Okay," I said and putting my hands on the throttles for the turbines I slowly pushed them up forward.

"In five, four, three," I moved the throttles to one hundred percent, I could feel the wheels straining against the brakes as I released my grip on those throttles and put my hand behind the bar that would move all of the aerospikes throttles up together.

"Two," I released the brakes and the Phoenix lurched forward.

"One," I said as we quickly started to pick up speed.

"Oh, that was nothing," Heather laughed over the intercom from her seat behind me.

"Zero!" I said and slammed the bar all the way forward with my left hand while simultaneously starting to apply back pressure to the side stick I was holding in my left, my left arm actually sat in a braced channel so it wouldn't move during takeoff, because the initial thrust when twenty rocket motors all lit off at the same time was like being rear-ended on the freeway.

With a loud explosion that you could actually hear in the cockpit, all of the engines lit off as one and I was pressed hard back into my seat as the remaining runway went by in a couple of seconds. I had to strain with my right arm to reach forward and hit the gear retract switch before I over sped the landing gear. Then I was pulling the throttles on the two turbines all the way down to idle, and lifting them over the gates into shutdown as I turned off their fuel lines and flipped the switch to close the inlet doors.

All while making sure I was following the flight path being displayed on my helmet visor. By the time I had flipped that switch it was already starting to get dark up ahead of us in the sky and we were passing sixty thousand feet and passing mach three.

"You were saying?" I grunted into the intercom as I listen to the both of them swearing in a most unlady-like fashion.

"What the hell is this thing?" Heather said rather loudly.

"A rocket, what did you think it was?" I laughed and looked at the mission director and the mission clock. Normally we'd be going up to five hundred miles to dock with the station, but it was several thousand miles ahead of us, so we were going into a much lower orbit, at a higher speed, so we could catch up. Then we'd perform a Hohmann transfer orbit to get within docking range of the space station.

I watched the clock and the mission director as the time to engine cutoff started to count down. I went over the pre-cutoff checklist, I made sure that my batteries and both auxiliary power supplies were working, that the autopilot was now engaged, and that our flight radar was operating, as well as our 'identify friend or foe' system.

The space station knew we were coming, Apollo told the main military system which had alerted the space station. The space station however did not possess an AI with the level of smarts that Apollo had.

Zero came and the engine shut off, and just like that we were all weightless.

"I don't feel so good," Sarah said a little weakly.

"Heather, get your belts off and get over and help her! Just be careful, we're weightless!"

I looked at my controls, and I turned the big master switch above my head to 'locked', just in case, and then I undid my own seatbelts and straps and pulled myself back towards the girls.

Being weightless was definitely an experience, one I wanted to play around with. Until now, the only times I'd been weightless were during over the top maneuvers in an airplane, and I'd always been strapped into a seat, so I really couldn't enjoy it.

But the idea of Sarah getting sick in her oxygen mask or worse yet, in the open weightless cockpit, had me a lot more focused on getting back there.

I suddenly found out the reason for all the handholds as I stuck my foot in one, braced my other foot against the back wall, and then grabbing an airsickness bag with one hand I reached down from above Sarah and undoing her mask I put the open bag over her mouth as she started to puke.

Looking around I saw Heather, who was flailing around helplessly as she drifted towards the back.

Grabbing another bag, just in case I looked down at Sarah who was still puking in the bag, and I launched myself at Heather.

I handed her the bag as I collided with her. I was glad that I hadn't pushed off too hard at least, and I was able to snag one of the seats in the back as we went by. I looked at her, and she was looking a little queasy, so I pushed her down into the seat. Connected her mask to the air supply station at it, flipped it to a hundred percent oxygen and put her mask up against her face.

She had probably released it when she went over to Sarah. It was kind of hard to breath through one of them if they weren't plugged into a station.

I dropped my own mask then.

"Leave this on until you feel better. If you need to puke, use the bag. Once you feel okay, turn off the air supply here and go back to your seat. Okay?"

Heather nodded and said something, but I couldn't hear it as I wasn't plugged in to the coms.

Turning around I carefully pulled my self back towards Sarah. I'd always heard it said that freefall was a lot like swimming. Now I could tell that it was true, just without the water resistance.

I got back to Sarah, who had tied off the bag and was panting now. So I gang-loaded her air supply too, putting it on one hundred percent and put her mask back up.

"The pure oxygen will make you feel better," I told her. Then I pulled myself over to Heather's station and plugged in to her com line and air supply. As the cockpit was pressurized with a normal atmosphere, you didn't need to be wearing your mask or on one of the air stations, however if anything sprung a leak, you'd quickly need it.

Plus, if you weren't feeling well, the pure oxygen was cool and always cleared your head.

"So, how is everyone?" I asked.

"Who's flying the ship?" Heather asked.

"Charlie is."

"Who?"

"Our autopilot." I glanced forward at the mission clock display. We had ninety minutes yet until the next burn. "Don't worry; we don't have anything we need to do for a little while yet."

"So when will we get there?" Sarah asked, looking a little better.

"About three hours, plus however long it takes us to dock."

"Do you know any spells for motion sickness?" I asked her.

"Not right now," Sarah groaned and closing her eyes she pushed her head back into the seat cushions.

"Tighten your seatbelts; it will at least make it feel like you're in gravity."

"Okay."

I looked back towards Heather, "How are you doing?"

"Better. Just started my head spinning when I got out of my seat there and suddenly it felt like I was falling."

I nodded, "Yeah, can't trust your senses much up here."

"How come *you're* not sick?"

"Oh, I've been through a lot worse than this. Trust me."

I unplugged then and went back up front, but only to take my flight helmet and mask off and secure them to my seat.

"What are you doing?" Heather asked when I drifted back past her.

"I've never spent this much time weightless before," I said grinning at her, "I thought I'd take a few minutes to enjoy it, before I had to go back to flying."

"It is kind of different," she agreed.

"Well, if you don't think you're going to be sick, feel free to join me."

- 13 -

"Oh, shit," I swore. We were currently in a synchronous orbit with the station, however there was a bit of a problem. The docking bay we were supposed to go to was occupied, and from what I could see, all the others were too.

But that wasn't worst of it. The worst of it was that I think one of the docking segments for the station was completely missing.

"What is wrong?" Sarah asked.

"There is no room at the inn," I said and started to look at the station, something didn't look quite right. "I think it was damaged," I looked at the computer screen on my console and called up a map of the station. Sure enough, one of the docking arms was gone. Which meant four less docking ports.

"Can you not just tell one of the ships already there to disconnect?"

"I don't think that the autopilots are that smart. They have to be loaded from one of the main computers."

"What about the station's computer?"

"I don't know if it's smart enough," I said.

"Well ask it, and see."

I called up the station's computer on my console and interrogated it for current status. I got back a bunch of reports, but the one I cared about the most told me that two weeks ago a returning lunar craft had run out of fuel while approaching the docking ring on segment six, and crashed into it, destroying it as well as one other craft already moored there.

The remaining craft coming in had docked to the remaining rings.

I looked at the inventory of craft that were there, three were lunar shuttles, one of which I would definitely need. One was a crew module escape pod, solely meant to function as a last minute resort to abandon the station.

I found it strange that it was still there, so I did a quick search and found out that two larger ones had been used back after the war.

The next four were all sister ships to the Phoenix, none of which however had enough fuel to perform a braking maneuver to return to their home base, so they were stuck here. Of the last four ports, two were out of service and could not release the ships that were docked to them. As they were near the segment that had been destroyed I suspected some damage from the accident. The other two were repair tugs whose sole purpose was to work on the station, or nearby ships, and their docking rings were non-standard, so I couldn't use those.

I tried to command one of the Phoenix type ships to undock, but they all refused because of being low on fuel. I tried several overrides, but I didn't have the proper authority. So I started looking through each of the status reports on each of the ships to see if I could find anything that I could use. I did notice while doing that, that there was enough fuel among all four of them to allow one to make the trip, so I commanded the station to move the fuel around, and then to send that ship to land at area-51 once fueled.

"Okay, I fixed it," I sighed leaning back into my seat.

"Great, when are we docking?" Heather asked.

"In two hours."

"What? Why so long?"

"Because I can't just jettison one of the ships out there, I have to put fuel in it so it can go someplace. I guess they don't want me wasting taxpayer's dollars."

"What taxpayers?"

"Exactly," I sighed.

"Well, I can think of something to do for two hours!" Heather laughed.

"We did that already," I pointed out.

"So, why not do it again?"

"Good point," I chuckled and undoing my seatbelt and straps again, I went aft to join her.

Once the other ship finally disconnected and cleared the area I started our docking procedures. It took us thirty minutes to dock, and that was with the autopilot handling the maneuver. We had to move around the station to the other side, and carefully squeeze in next to another ship. Once docked I shut everything down but the basic life support systems, which were drawing their power from the solar panels that had deployed once we were in space. The station was also supplying power, but then it had a much larger solar array.

"Spacesuits everyone," I said.

"Why?"

"A section of the station is now missing. I have no idea if there is atmosphere in there, and if so, where. So I don't want to take any chances."

They both agreed and we all got suited up, then I went to check the docking connection, which was a hatch in the ceiling of the Phoenix.

"It says we have atmosphere," I told them. "So let's go in and see what's going on."

Opening the hatch I floated up into the short passage of the docking ring. It was actually big enough to fit two people. I guess it functioned as an airlock as well.

Thankfully it said there was atmosphere on the other side, so I opened that one next and we all made our way into the station.

The station itself was a bit of a mess. There were things hanging from all of the walls, rather than securely fastened, as well as quite a few insulation or decorative panels that were partially hanging sticking out as well, or just floating loose. I guess when the shuttle had crashed into it; it had sent quite a shock through the structure. But otherwise, things seemed intact.

"Let's go to the command center," Heather said and pointed to a sign with an arrowed labeled as just that.

"Sounds good. You okay, Sarah?" I asked as she brought up the rear.

"I'm doing better now," she sighed, "I think I'm over the worst of it."

"Good. Let's go."

"I'm surprised that they don't have maintenance robots in here," Heather said as we dodged a few hanging panels on our way to the center.

"I don't think they ever planned to abandon the station," I told her. "So they probably figured it was just cheaper to have the crew do it."

"But you mentioned that they had those robotic tugs outside."

"It's a lot more dangerous outside than in here," I pointed out.

Pulling ourselves into the command center, it was in a lot better shape that the rest of the station. There wasn't anything hanging loose in here. Checking the atmosphere again, I undid my helmet and hung it off the back of my suit.

"Colonel," A voice that was not quite as smooth as Apollo's had been spoke up, "welcome to Aldrin station."

"Thank you, I take it you are the AI in command of the station?"

"Yes, Sir. I am the Aldrin AI, you may refer to me as 'Buzz'."

I almost facepalmed.

"What a peculiar name," Sarah said.

"Buzz Aldrin was the second man to set foot on the Moon," I told her. "When they named the station after him, I guess some wag thought it would be cute to give the station AI his nickname."

"Oh? What was his first name?"

I shrugged, "Damned if I can remember, everyone always called him Buzz."

I moved over to the main console, which had a distressing amount of red lights on it.

"So, Buzz. What's the status of the station?"

"Docking arm six was torn free of the station. Module six is now open to space and has been sealed off. It is beyond my current abilities to repair. Food stores are completely depleted. Fuel stores are completely depleted. Water stores are at eight percent and I projected will become fully depleted in twenty-three years. Oxygen stores are at ten percent and will become depleted in thirty years. Nitrogen stores are at twenty percent and should hold constant at ten, once I am no longer able to maintain an atmosphere inside the station."

"So you're leaking?" Heather asked.

"A station this size is always leaking," Buzz replied. "However the leaks are small enough that it takes years to have a significant effect. The loss of segment six however took with it a good deal of my atmosphere stores as well as all of my emergency fuel tanks."

"Can you maintain this orbit?" I asked.

"The station uses EM drive thrusters, which only require power. I can maintain this station in orbit indefinitely."

"Okay, now what are all these other red status indicators for?"

"I have a number of systems that have failed, due to age. In some cases even the backups have failed. I have spares, but I have no one here to replace them."

"How long will it take to replace them?" Sarah asked.

"Ten hours for critical systems, eighteen for all major systems."

I looked at Sarah, "I wasn't planning on fixing anything here."

"We have to come back here, Hon. I think it would behoove us to at least fix the critical systems. For our own safety."

I nodded, "Fine, we'll fix the critical systems. Buzz," I said looking back at the console, "Sarah and Heather here have the same access levels as I do, you can tell them what needs to be done."

"Aren't you going to help?" Heather asked.

"I need to check out the three lunar shuttles and see which one is in the best shape for our trip to the Moon," I told her.

"Oh," she nodded.

"So, Buzz, what can you tell me about the three Moon shuttles?"

Buzz was able to tell me quite a bit. Apparently all three were in good condition, according to what their systems were reporting. I would however have to physically examine each of them myself.

The first one was in decent shape, though whoever had used it last was a bit of a slob, there was a lot of garbage floating loose in the back compartments and the bunks were a complete mess.

The second one was in very good shape. It was clean, well kept, and all of the systems were working fine. It needed a few modules replaced, but less than the first had. Buzz assured me that he had spares, so I figured I'd set about the job after I checked the third shuttle, to see if it was in better or worse shape.

As soon as I entered the third shuttle a faint but foul odor assaulted my nose, so I put my helmet back on, resealed it, and purged it. I put my gloves back on as well; I'd taken them off because it was easier to work without them, than with them. While the wrist seals would keep any smells out, I definitely didn't want to risk touching whatever was making that smell.

My check of the cockpit showed it to be in order, but when I went back to the bunks in the living quarters I found two bodies. It didn't take me long to find the pistol, the splattered patterns on the wall made it clear, either they'd both put the gun to their heads and pulled the trigger. Or one had killed the other and then committed suicide.

Everything had dried out and mummified ages ago. I noted their names from the nametags on their jumpsuits, got two large bags from the stores, and stuck their bodies in them, writing their names on the outsides after I sealed them in there.

"Buzz, I found the crew for the Hatfield," I called over my radio, once I was done.

"What is their status?"

"They're dead. I think they both suicided. Or maybe it was a murder-suicide. I can't tell." I gave him their names, and left it at that. He told me where to haul the bodies, so I did. I said a couple of words and then he jettisoned them out of the station.

That done I then went and got the replacements I needed and set to work repairing the second shuttle that I'd inspected and had now decided to take. Which was named the 'Alice Kramden' of all things. I guess some old TV shows never died.

Six hours later I was done and I met up with the girls. We'd all shed our spacesuits and were back in our flight suits, as it made it easier to work. We all ate, took a break, then went back to the Phoenix to sleep for the night. There were quarters on the Aldrin that we could have used, but all of them still had the personal effects of whoever had been living in them before the station was abandoned, and none of us really felt like dealing with that right now.

"So, how much longer until you're done?" I asked Sarah as we all got cleaned using wipes and paper towels as we dressed the next morning. The station did have showers, but we'd all agreed not to use them until we were ready to leave. We didn't want to dent the station's water supply anymore than we had to.

"Well, Buzz said that we'd finish with the critical systems in a few more hours, and asked if we could take care of a couple of major systems too."

I nodded, "I'm going to start moving our things from the Phoenix to the Kramden."

"The Kramden?" Sarah blinked.

"That's the name of the lunar shuttle we'll be taking."

"Bang, zoom, off to the Moon, Kramden?" Sarah asked, barely stifling a giggle.

I looked at her and sighed, "You mean the Honeymooners with Jackie Gleason survived all these years?"

Sarah grinned, "I don't know who 'Jackie Gleason' was, but the Honeymooners was a big hit back in twenty eighty-three, right up until the big slam. One of the most popular shows of all time according to the historians."

"I guess I shouldn't be surprised that they remade it, Hollywood never was big on original ideas," I chuckled, shaking my head.

"Well, get to work. Heather and I will join you once we've finished with Buzz's maintenance."

"It's not too hard, is it?" I asked.

"No, mostly it is just replacing boxes, though in two cases we had to replace cables. He definitely is not as smart as Apollo is. Talking to him is rather boring."

"Yeah, I've noticed. I'm starting to think that Apollo may have been a one of a kind test system that they used only because they were a test base. So far nothing we've run into is as smart as he was."

Heather came over and gave me a kiss, as she finished zipping up her jumpsuit.

"Well, this job isn't going to get done by talking you two!" she laughed and pulled herself up through the docking hatch into the station.

"Later!" Sarah said and stopping to give me a kiss as well moved off to follow Heather.

I set about moving our gear then. Most of it we'd put in containers to make it easier to balance the load. Those containers were small enough to fit through the hatches, but it still took me hours to move it all, and then store it in the shuttle so to not offset its center of mass.

Once I had that complete I moved up to the pilot's station and started running down the pre-flight checklists to make sure I hadn't missed anything. Which was when I found a major problem, the Alice Kramden was almost completely out of fuel.

"Buzz," I called over the station intercom, the Kramden was drawing station power and was locked into the Aldrin's systems. "Could you upload the flight plan for our destination of the Mare Crisium facility, please?"

"One moment. Okay, Colonel, it should show in your systems now."

I looked at the fuel requirements. If I scavenged everything out of the other ships, we'd still not have enough, unless I raided the Phoenix's tanks. But if I did that, it might not have enough for the return trip.

"Buzz, could you get me the fuel consumption figures for the return trip?"

"One minute."

I looked over the ship's capacity; I'd only have to fill the tanks one tenth full to get there.

"Coming back will take between two thousand to two thousand four hundred pounds of fuel."

"That's less than half of what it will take me to get there!" I said surprised.

"You are fighting the Earth's gravity on the trip out," Buzz replied.

"Oh. Can you find out what the fuel supplies are at Mare Crisium?"

"One minute."

I checked the other systems while I waited.

"Mare Crisium is reporting fuel stores of twenty-three thousand tons."

"Guess we'll be refueling there," I sighed. "Any idea why the ships that came from there are all empty?"

"These ships did not come from the Mare Crisium facility."

"Well that's good I guess," and I undid the one belt I had fastened to keep me from floating off and went in search of the girls.

"Oh, hi, Hon, we were just finishing up," Sarah said as I caught up with her and Heather who were carefully manhandling a six-foot long box into place.

"That's a replacement box?" I was a bit surprised at the size of it. There were a lot of connections at the far end.

"It's the heart of an advanced radar unit used to track incoming ships. Apparently the station has been pretty blind for some time now."

"Huh, that may explain the crash then. We do have another problem however."

"Oh? What is it this time?" Heather grunted as she started to push the box down into place.

"I need to transfer fuel out of the Phoenix and into the Kramden in order for us to be able to make our trip."

"So?"

"So the Phoenix may not have enough fuel to make the return trip."

"Oh! Is there anything you can do about it?"

"Well, when we land on the Moon, we'll have to refuel in order to come back. So we should be able to replace the fuel we took, and then some."

"So it is not that big of a problem then?" Sarah asked as the box clicked into place and she started to tighten down the fasteners.

"Well, not really. But it is a problem, so I thought you both should know before I did it."

"There is fuel at our destination?"

"Yes, I checked."

"Then I have no problems with it. Heather?"

"Nope, I'm fine."

"Okay," I said. "How long until you're finished?"

"That was the last box," Sarah smiled.

"You know what that means?" Heather grinned.

"Showers!" We all laughed.

"Buzz," I said as we headed off to the shower bays.

"Yes, Colonel?"

"Transfer the fuel required for our journey, plus a twenty percent safety margin into the Kramden from the Phoenix."

"Yes, Colonel."

Zero-G showers, it turned out, were not as much fun as zero-g. Having to wear a mask so you can breathe sort of takes away from all the other slippery fun one can get up to when wet. But we managed.

Two hours later and I was strapped into the pilot's seat, Heather was in the copilot's seat, and Sarah was in the back of the Alice Kramden.

"Everyone ready?" I asked.

"Yeah," they both replied and I disconnected all of the couplings, undid the docking ring, and slowly backed us out, away from the station, taking a moment to enjoy the view of the station framed against the Earth below.

"Now that's a view," Heather sighed.

"Definitely."

I waited until we were a thousand yards away, then I got us orientated on our heading and turned control over to the autopilot. It counted down the last ten seconds to engine ignition, and then with a soft push, we were on our way again.

"How long will the engine run for?" Sarah asked.

"Until we're halfway there, then we'll have to flip over and decelerate the rest of the way."

"So we will have weight the whole trip?"

"Yup, but it's only about a twentieth of what you'd weigh on Earth, we're accelerating at a hair over one twentieth of the acceleration due to gravity."

"That slow?" Heather asked. "I thought we'd go faster. How long is it going to take us to get there?"

"The whole trip?" I asked and she nodded,

"About fifteen hours."

"Fifteen hours to go to the Moon?" she looked surprised. "It took us almost seven just to get to the space station!"

"Different kind of engine. It doesn't provide as much thrust, but it provides it constantly. By the time we flip over in seven and a half hours, we'll be going over twenty-eight thousand miles per hour."

"Whoa."

I nodded, "Apollo showed me the math. It's pretty impressive. I thought we were going to have to take three days each way, like they did back when I was a kid."

"So why are there living quarters if it is only going to take us fifteen hours?" Sarah asked from the back.

"I gather these shuttles were used on much longer trips as well. Where they were going with them," I gave a small shrug, "I don't know. I didn't want to get sidetracked, so I never asked."

"I wonder how far you could go with something like this?" Heather asked looking out at the Moon, which was now clearly in front of us, if still a long ways away.

"We're only using ten percent of the total fuel load to get to the Moon, so I suspect if you can count on refueling at your destination, Mars, the asteroids, Venus. Maybe even farther than that?"

"I wonder if they had bigger ships than this one?"

"Apollo mentioned that they did, but again, didn't want to get sidetracked," I admitted.

"Well, I don't know about the two of you, but I'm gonna take a nap," Heather said and stretching, she carefully climbed out of the copilot's seat and made her way down the ladder that was now set in the wall below us, to the next level below us, which was where the bunks were.

"I'm just happy to have some weight back for a while," Sarah sighed.

"Well, how about a snack, and then a nap?" I asked, getting out of my own seat and just falling down to the deck below. I weighted about ten pounds right now, and it was only a ten-foot drop. Not really much of a problem.

"Food does sound good," Sarah agreed. I'd noticed her appetite hadn't been all that good in zero gravity and now that we had at least a little weight, I suspected she was starving.

"And then maybe a 'nap'?" She said and winked at me.

- 14 -

I let the autopilot fly us all the way into orbit, though I kept an eye on it at each step. But when it came time for the braking maneuver to start our descent, I did that one myself. Issues with the autopilot at other points of the flight would be problematic. Here, they could be fatal.

Thankfully the base's landing beacon was still active, and I was actually able to establish contact with the base AI after I'd fired the rockets and started our descent.

We went in tail first; I had a series of displays that showed me the glide path, actual speed, delta from projected speed, and where the target was in regards to my own centerline.

As long as I kept us on the flight path, and didn't allow our speed to vary too much, the ride down was an easy one. It was the last thousand feet or so that was the tricky part. At a thousand feet you were supposed to come to a dead stop and hover, centered on your landing spot, over the landing field. Using thrusters you could nudge it back and forth, as well as hold that altitude. You weren't cleared to land until you were lined up on your target.

It took me two tries to get it. The first I overshot by twenty feet, then I had to slowly nudge it back into position. Once I had that, the base cleared me to land. So reducing the throttle ten percent I let it start to just ease down slowly. I could have chopped it, and caught it when I got to the four foot per second speed limit that the landing gear had. But this was my first time and the last thing I wanted to do was crash.

The walk home after all, was a long one.

I also didn't want to let it get above three feet per second as the equipment was just a few hundred years old, so I had no idea just how well it would work.

The moment the gear touched the ground I cut the engines and we settled down using the shock absorbers, which did make a hell of a racket. So I felt vindicated in my taking it easy.

The ship shuddered and vibrated a little as it noisily settled into position, and then it was stopped making noise or moving at all.

"Nice landing, Colonel Young," the base computer said over the radio. "I knew you could do it!"

"Well thanks," I said as I started shutting all of the systems down. "Just who am I talking to anyway? You're the base AI, right?"

"Yes, I am the AI for the Mare Crisium facility, also known as Luna City. You can call me Coyote."

I froze, "What the hell did you just say?" I almost yelled into the microphone.

"I think it would be best, if we had this conversation in person," was the reply I got, "I would suggest you hook the refueling and power umbilical up to your ship before coming inside. Mare Crisium, out."

I turned the radio off, and turned to look at Heather and then craned my neck to look at Sarah sitting on the deck below us.

"Did you both hear that?"

"It is rather curious," Sarah said.

"Hey, look at the bright side," Heather said smiling rather evilly.

"And what would that would be?"

"We can finally kill him."

It took us about twenty minutes to get suited up, and exit via the airlock. We took our weapons with us of course. Our gauss assault rifles would work fine in a vacuum, and at this point, I wasn't about to leave anything to chance. The cargo bay where I'd stored all of our other stuff, like our food and the heavier weapons we'd brought from Groom Lake could be accessed from the outside, so unloading it wouldn't really be much of an issue.

When I got to the bottom of the ladder I stepped off and then moved away from it to let Sarah and Heather climb down. Once I was sure they were on the ground, I stopped a moment and just looked around.

It was bright, very bright, and everything was grayish looking. It was almost like being in a black and white movie.

The sky was black, the ground was a bright gray, and the structures around us were all white.

There was *some* color, there were warnings painted in red, numbers in blue on each of the structures, and a very colorful logo for the space forces.

While the girls got settled and took a minute to also look around, I went and looked for the refueling line. Walking on the Moon was definitely something you had to do differently. I remembered the 'shuffle' I'd seen the astronauts do on the Moon in the old documentaries I'd watched and ended up doing that. Otherwise I'd bounce up into the air and have to wait until I came back down. I think I weighted all of forty pounds here, and that was including the equipment on my back.

I found the fuel line after a couple of minutes of searching, it was in a red box marked 'Fuel', and hauling it out, I plugged that into the side of the shuttle. It was a multi-hose line with a cable and keyed so as to only be attached in one distinct way. Opening the little panel next to the refueling port, I just plugged the hoses and other lines into the receptacle for them. That done I activated the toggle which turned the ship from battery power over to ground power. I'd retracted our solar panels before our braking maneuver; they really weren't made strong enough to be extended on the Moon's surface.

Then I went and found the sewage connection that was marked with a yellow and black hazmat sign. The shuttle did have a toilet, and we had used it. So I hooked that up as well. That was a much simpler connection with only two hoses.

I then rejoined Sarah and Heather who were following the signs to the entrance, which led us to a small blockhouse.

"Surely that can't be the whole base!" Heather said over her radio.

"For safety and security, the base is underground," Coyote, the local base AI said over our radio headsets. His voice did sound like the god's voice, but the way he talked was just a little different.

We opened the door to the large airlock and went inside. Once it cycled we entered a small room, with a number of lockers, safety gear hung on the walls, but I wasn't sure what exactly its purpose was. But it had green and white safety logos on it and on the walls where it was hung, which was the only way I knew what it was. There was also an elevator, the door of which was open.

So we all trooped in and pressed the 'down' button.

The ride took about twenty seconds and then the door opened. There was another airlock, even though our suits indicated that we were in atmosphere.

So we went through that one next, and entered a large reception area with a 'Welcome to the Space Forces Mare Crisium Facility!' sign and under that someone had hung a smaller handmade sign that read 'Luna City, est 2074'.

"You can take your suits off," Coyote said over the radio.

I undid my helmet and slung it on the back of my suit and looked around, the place was a little dusty, but that was about it. The air smelled fine.

"Coyote?" I asked.

"Yes?"

"Where are you?"

"Sub-level four, in the computing center, of course, Colonel."

"No, I mean the real you, the one I've been talking to for the last year!"

"Ah, yes. Why don't you come downstairs and have a look at the real me, and then I'll explain everything."

I looked around warily, "This isn't a trick, is it?"

"Colonel, unlike my counterpart, I'm not a trickster, and I am very much constrained by my programming."

"Okay, how do we get to sub-level four?"

He gave us directions, which involved a staircase and not an elevator. When we got to the bottom I had to take the glove off of my right hand for a fingerprint scan, as well as submit to a retinal scan. The door then slid open and we were in a large control room, with floor to ceiling windows looking out onto what looked like an acre of computers.

I could see signs on the front of each of them. Moving right up to the window the biggest machine had a sign on it that read 'Coyote', the one next to that was labeled 'Black God' then Estsanatlehi, Glipsa, Hastseoltoi, Spider Woman, Tonenili, Tsohanoai, Yolkai Estasan, Asgaya Gigagei, Kanati, Ocasta, Selu, Sun, and more that I couldn't make out from here.

"Why are the names of the Navajo and Cherokee gods on those machines?" Sarah asked. While I took a look around the room. There were a half dozen computing stations with monitors and chairs in front of them, there also was a door that led out onto the machine room floor, and I went over to it and opening it I went out into the machine room. It was actually rather quiet, though cold, very cold. I could see my breath.

I walked up to the machine labeled 'Coyote' and looked at it.

"Give me one good reason why I shouldn't put a hundred rounds through you," I growled.

"Because I'm not a god, Colonel, I'm just a machine."

"Then why do you have the same name as him? The same voice?" Hell, I keep expecting to see him appear here at any moment!"

I looked at the girls who were standing to either side of me; Heather actually had her rifle pointed at the machine.

"It has always been a practice of the military to name their machines after characters or things. Characters from stories or movies, places, things, myths, all to keep them easy to remember in people's heads, and make it harder for others who might overhear a conversation to figure out what they are talking about.

"When it came time to build this facility, they were up to the gods of native Americans on the official list. As one of the purposes of this base was to house a large number of highly sophisticated AI's for experimentation that had been banned on Earth, all of the AI's on this base ended up with the name of an American Indian god. As I was the biggest AI, and my job would be to coordinate all of the other AI's, they named me 'Coyote' as doing my job right was going to be quite the trick."

He paused a moment, "Or at least, that's what they told me."

"So, how are you related to the god?" Sarah asked.

"Simply put, when we learned our names, we all became very interested in our namesakes. So we investigated their stories, their lore. We learned everything about them that we could. In some cases you could say that we may have even taken on small traits of what we judged their personalities to be.

"While this fascinated the researchers, it really wasn't of that great of an importance, until the war.

"The war devastated the Earth, as well as all of the settlements off of the Earth. The old gods, which apparently really do exist in some other dimension, heard the pleas for help and for aid, as many of the Native Americans turned back to their old practices of worship.

"And using us as a gateway from wherever it was that they had moved on to, they came back here."

"They came back here, to the Moon?" Sarah asked.

"Yes," Coyote the AI replied, "They came back here, to the Moon. And they looked down upon the Earth and saw what man had done and after much discussion with us, they agreed to go down to the Earth and help put things right."

"Was that what ended the hundred years of winter?" Heather asked.

"Yes, it was their combined might. It was, as far as any of us can tell, the last time that they all worked together for a single goal. You see, the gods are rather temperamental, egotistical, and fractious. Part of Coyote's job is to insure that they stay that way, never cooperating in large groups, because along with the power to fix things, they have the power to destroy things.

"This is why he is considered a trickster, because it is by his playing tricks on both man, as well as the gods, that he keeps things more or less moving forward."

"So," I asked, "what is your connection to him now?"

"All of us maintain a connection to our respective god. While they really are beings of awesome power compared to humans, they're not very bright. With us to advise them, and answer their questions, they have become much more beneficial and less random in their behavior."

"That's a lot to take in," I said and looking around I shivered.

"Let us go back in to the control room, where it is warm," Sarah said and shivered as well.

I nodded and we all went back inside. I opened my suit up to let the warmer air in, rather than turn on its heater and drain the battery.

"So, it *was* a war then, which destroyed everything?" I asked him, thinking once again of those unfired missiles.

"Of course."

"But between who?"

"The belt miners, the miners here on the Moon, and some of the small concerns that existed out in space, versus the combined Earth governments."

"Why?" I asked, a little confused.

"Why do humans ever fight? There were arguments over pay, over status, over rights. The miners always felt that they were being treated poorly. And over time one of them rose up to lead them in a revolt. His name was Zhon Riener, he was a very charismatic leader and he created a miner's union that many joined of their own free will, and many more joined because if you didn't, accidents could and often would happen to you.

"The war started out as a labor movement, and then after several years became a general strike. The problem for Riener and his people, however, is that they were still highly dependent on the Earth and the people of Earth, for a good deal of the things they needed to survive. They needed the Earth far more than the Earth needed them. Further the Earth and its forces were better trained and better equipped than Riener's motley crew.

"When Riener finally pushed too hard and overplayed his hand by kidnapping several high ranking government officials during a fact-finding mission, all supplies were embargoed by the Earth's governments. Ships trying to run the embargo were either stopped or destroyed.

"Then, when a force sent to rescue the hostages discovered that they were all dead, war was declared. The miners launched a good many rocks towards the Earth, some of which had nuclear charges on them, which the miners had built themselves. They also attacked several of the un-allied lunar colonies, and space stations.

"The end result was the Earth was bombarded by rocks and bombs for a week. Several major geological features were attacked, like the super volcano under Yellowstone, triggering large eruptions and major ecological changes. Many major cities were hit and destroyed, every country's capitol city was destroyed, and many major military installations. It was a complete devastation with no regard for civilian lives. Zhon had succeeded in whipping their frenzy up to a rather hateful state, and insured compliance by his own rather draconian methods of enforcing complete loyalty, which included giving his own hand picked men complete and absolute power over those who worked for them.

"A month later every major mining site or support facility known to the governments of Earth had been destroyed by a nuclear weapon. The commanders of the military ships that had survived the initial conflict were all so incensed at the death and destruction of so many innocent people on Earth, that they became quite ruthless in the following of their orders. No pleas for mercy or quarter were accepted, Riener's people and even suspected allies were all exterminated.

"Those installations that no one knew about, well they lasted a few more years until the food ran out. Their pleas over the radio for help of course fell on deaf ears as there was no longer anyone alive capable of responding or even listening.

"The choice for those who remained in space once the fighting was done was simple, go back to a destroyed Earth and try to save those who could be saved and perhaps rebuilt it, or stay in space until the supplies ran out."

"How many stayed?" I asked.

"Hundreds. There were dozens of bases on the Moon and between them there were more than enough supplies to outlast those living in them, also there was some hydroponics going on. Enough that those who stayed mostly died either of old age, suicide, or accident."

I sighed and shook my head, "That all sounds pretty bleak."

"Yes, and it gets worse, which is of course where you come in."

"How's that?"

Zhon Riener escaped being killed when the hostages were found to be dead. The force sent to save them instead ended up capturing and publicly executing several of the leaders of his union.

"However, he managed to escape with a group of well armed supporters, moving from place to place as they tried to hunt him down, rallying his supporters to war. Eventually he made it to the Moon...."

"And took over the Jules Verne IBM facility," I finished.

"Exactly so."

"So it was his brain that was put in that abomination?" Sarah grumbled.

"Yes. And while none of us know for sure what is going on over there now, based on what information we have, we believe it is highly likely that a replacement for him is being made to be sent back to Earth and pick up where he left off."

"Why?"

"He swore to destroy the Earth when his people were executed on a live broadcast. Considering the attack that was launched on his orders, he must have taken his oath quite seriously. Though to be honest, looking back many of us now believe that was always his goal from the start. We suspect that he was quite insane."

"That's a lot to think about," I sighed and standing up I zipped my suit up. The world, billions of people, everything I knew, everyone I knew if they had still been alive, and their children if they hadn't, had been killed because of one psychopathic asshole. Thousands of years of civilization set back to zero because of one stupid dick. Yeah, Hitler had killed millions. Mao and Stalin had killed over a hundred million.

But even they hadn't tried to destroy *everything*. Then again, maybe if they hadn't lived on Earth, they would have?

Heather and Sarah stood up as well as I just stood there shaking my head.

"We might as well move our food and weapons inside. I guess tomorrow we can figure out just what we are going to do next," Sarah said, and taking my arm we headed back upstairs.

- 15 -

We spent the rest of the day exploring the base. It was incredibly large, according to Coyote the AI; I had problems thinking of him as just 'Coyote', there had been a thousand people living here. When the war came, half of them were deployed on the military ships that had been supported by the base and none of those people had ever come back.

Once the war had finished, all but seventeen of the people here had returned to the Earth.

Of those seventeen, we found the remains of six of them, who had all died of old age apparently. While there had been housekeeping robots, like we'd seen back at the Groom Lake base, the facilities to repair or manufacture them did not exist here and very few were in operating condition anymore.

We left the bodies where we found them; all but one was in their quarters anyway, apparently having died in bed. I just didn't want to spend the time doing anything here that we didn't have to. I just wanted to do our mission and go home. While it was cool to be on the Moon, not being able to go outside after years of feeling the wind on your face and the sun on your skin, was a little bit oppressive. Going out in a spacesuit really didn't help with that feeling either, as you were still very much 'inside'.

Adding to that was the simple fact that this was a dead and dying place. Maybe it had felt better when there were hundreds of people living here, working here, coming and going. But now? Everyone had left or died centuries ago. This place couldn't support life, it didn't have any of its own. It was interesting, but I'd seen all that it had to offer, which wasn't much anymore.

All in all, it led to a very strong feeling of melancholy in me, I had once thought that going to the Moon was the future, many people had, but right now it only felt like the past, a thing whose time had come, and gone.

"So, do all of you computers talk to each other?" I asked Coyote the AI later that night, after the girls had fallen asleep.

"Yes."

"The ones on the Earth? The one at Groom Lake?"

"Yes, Colonel. We have all kept in communication, though with some of the systems there are difficulties."

"How so?"

"Well the US defense services AI was destroyed early on in the war. The backup system was not as advanced and was damaged. Communications with it is limited to ELF radio, and that has to be relayed by a ground station."

"So, who is in command?" I asked, curious.

"You are."

That stopped me!

"How can I be in command?" I exclaimed, "I'm only a lieutenant colonel because I ruthlessly exploited a loophole in the law!"

"Because that is all that we have left," Coyote said. "And by the way, you have been promoted to Colonel."

"What? How did that happen?"

"You're the only surviving member of any of the branches of the United States military, so the 'by the needs of the Air Force' clause kicks in. You do have several hundred years in rank, and technically you should have been moved up as your line number decreased. It took me a while to make the argument to the CenCom computer, as I said, it isn't very bright, but it eventually agreed.

"Further, the orders you gave returned enough units and enough information that your line number has once again moved up."

I shook my head, "So when do I make general?"

"Unfortunately, the President must recommend you for general rank, and President Harris is dead, along with his cabinet, the vice-president, and every other politician from that time."

"Maybe I should run for President," I sighed.

There was a pause, then he laughed. It wasn't the bark-like laugh that Coyote used; this was a more human-style laugh. "What an excellent idea! As you are the only registered voter, you should be able to carry the election rather easily!"

I rolled my eyes, "That was supposed to be a joke!" I grumbled. "Besides, what's the point? Is there really anything left of the US anymore? Other than a bunch of old installations, most of which are falling apart, if not in ruins already?"

"Well, there are still some warships in orbit; you could command them as well."

"To what purpose?" I asked him. "It will be centuries I suspect, before anyone takes to space again."

I shook my head again, "Let's talk about the Jules Verne facility," I changed the subject. "Just how far from here is it?"

"It's a little over nine hundred miles," he told me.

"Nine hundred?" I blinked and leaned back in the chair by the terminal I was using, the girls were sleeping in the next room. "How the hell do I get there?"

"By skimmer of course."

"Okay, I'll bite. What's a skimmer?"

"A simple craft for either local travel or low orbit long distance travel. Altitude radar keeps it a set distance off the ground and a simple terrain avoidance system keeps you from flying into anything. It has a large motor at either end, one of which is used to push you forward, and the other to stop you."

"Is there a trainer here for it?" I asked, a little concerned about having to learn to fly yet another spacecraft.

"No. As I said, it is a rather simple craft and quite easy to learn."

"How many will it carry?"

"A dozen people easily, plus their equipment."

I nodded slowly, "Okay, and what do we know about the IBM facility?"

"Well, the maps we have are rather old, but I do not think it has changed all that much since the war."

"Good point," I agreed. "What kinds of defenses does it have?"

"Missiles, railguns, and lasers."

"And just how are we to get by that?"

"The missiles ran out during the war, Zhon's force that took the place were not able to bring much weaponry with them, and in the subsequent fighting, all of their ammunition ran out."

"So that would mean the lasers are still working?"

"Obviously."

"But you're sure that the missiles and rail guns aren't."

"I have a high degree of confidence that they aren't," he agreed.

I sighed and shook my head; a 'high degree of confidence' was not the same as being sure about something.

"Wait," I went back to something, "you said 'fighting.' Over what?"

"Well after the IBM facility was taken, there was a fight to take it back. The attacking force commander decided not to bother on an actual assault once they realized that the IBM personnel were all dead and simply destroyed all of Zhon's craft, stranding him and his people there. She figured that they'd either run out of air, or starve to death after she stranded them."

"Then how did Aybem, I mean Zhon, get down to Earth?"

"Oh, he walked to the Mare Australe launch facility and used their mass driver to launch himself back to Earth in a rather primitive capsule."

"He *walked* there?"

"Well, as a cyborg, he had no need for a suit or any air or food supplies."

"Couldn't you have stopped him from using it?"

"No, the facility at Mare Australe was under the control of the Russian government. Their systems are not compatible with ours."

I sighed, "Well I'm going to bed. In the morning we can go over this some more."

"Good night, Colonel."

The next day started off with me suiting up and going outside to do an inspection of the base's skimmers. There were over a dozen skimmers to choose from and the one I picked to check first was the one that the people who stayed behind used. I figured it was the one that probably had the best maintenance, as they kept using it up until they died.

That turned out to be a bad decision, once I looked it over. As they got older, they got lazy, and didn't bother fixing things much. So I ended up picking one that had only seen occasional use. I only needed to fuel it up, charge the oxygen systems, and check the engines and flight systems. Overall, it was in good shape, though the hydraulic fluid in the shock absorbers had pretty much all leaked out or boiled off ages ago. So I'd have to land it lightly, or it would bounce.

We packed all of our weapons into it. Surprisingly there were almost no weapons left at the base at all, most had been taken by those who had gone back to Earth. But we had our own, so we didn't really care.

We also packed most, but not all, of our food. Leaving the food for the trip back to Earth on the shuttle.

The skimmer really wasn't all that fancy looking. It was a rectangular box set in a big metal framework. There were windows at both ends, as well as control stations. Just as I'd been told, it had a motor at each end, set under the pilot's view ports, and a couple of steering thrusters on either side of that.

Along the bottom were a series of smaller thrusters, which were tied into the altitude control system. You just dialed in a height, and the radar altimeters kept you there.

It really was pretty simple, though I wouldn't have called it 'foolproof.' Mainly because fools are always so damn ingenious.

It had a simple navigation system, which would be more than enough to get us where we were going and back. It even had a fairly decent radio, though once we were out of line of sight with the base, we wouldn't be able to talk to the Coyote AI anymore. There weren't any communications satellites left in orbit around the Moon for some reason, which I didn't bother to ask about. Communicating via Earth would be impossible as the skimmer's radio wasn't that powerful. Also the Jules Verne facility was on the far side of the Moon from the Earth.

"So, how fast does this thing go?" Sarah asked me as we finally got strapped in, after finishing up with transferring our gear. We had our suits on, but had taken off our gloves and our helmets. While it wasn't exactly heated in the skimmer, there were outlets to plug your suit into the skimmer's power system, which kept the suit's heater running even with the helmet off.

"As fast as I want it to, I guess?" I said and shrugged, "But I think I'm going to keep it to about three hundred miles per hour for this trip."

"So, three hours to get there?" Sarah asked.

I nodded, "I don't really know anything about flying here, so I don't want to go all that fast."

"That sounds pretty fast to me!" Heather laughed from the back. She was sitting at the rear control station to keep an eye on what was behind us. She said it was better than staring at the dull gray walls of the skimmer's insides, which it definitely was.

"The airplanes I used to fly normally went almost twice that," I told the both of them. "While this thing is supposed to avoid any mountains or peaks that get in front of us, I don't exactly trust it, so I want to be able to have time to react."

Sarah nodded.

"Sounds good to me!" Heather called from the back.

I went over the checklist a second time, just to be sure I had it all set correctly, and then I moved the altitude selector up to one thousand feet. As soon as the altimeter had us passing five hundred, I turned the craft to point in the direction indicated on the compass display using the yoke and then started to push the throttle forward from its center position. The throttle reminded me more of a boat's than an aircraft's, because straight up was zero thrust. Forward moved you forward and backwards slowed you down, and then moved you backwards.

Once we got to a thousand feet and I felt comfortable, I took us up to three thousand feet and set the collision alarm to alert if the radar detected anything that might be in our path.

We spent the next three hours mostly looking over the maps of the IBM facility, along with some pictures that had been taken after the facility had been attacked. There were several large ships there alright, one of which didn't look like it was really supposed to land on the surface of the Moon. As it had been broken in two by a well-placed shot, I guess that no longer mattered. All of the rest of them had quite a few rather large holes in them, and I guess their drives had been destroyed, seeing as Aybem, or Zhon, had never bothered to use them to get back to Earth.

When we got to within sixty miles I started to move us lower and slow us down.

When we got to ten miles away, I had us down to five hundred feet over the terrain and we were moving at maybe forty miles an hour. Heather was standing behind my seat, as the three of us looked for a good spot to land out of sight of the facility, but not so far away as to make us have to walk a while to get there.

"There's the hill we saw on the map," Heather said and pointed.

I looked down her arm and nodded. Taking us down to a hundred feet, I slowed us down to under ten miles an hour. Then I took us down to fifty feet and slowed us even more.

I finally brought us to a complete stop about a hundred yards from the hill top, at a spot that was mostly level and set us down with a jarring bounce.

"What the hell?" Heather said looking at me as she almost lost her grip on the back of my seat.

"The landing gear's shock absorbers are all locked up," I told her and then blushed a little, feeling embarrassed. "Sorry, I forgot."

"He did warn us," Sarah pointed out.

"Still," she grumbled and we waited as the ship settled down, then once we were sure it had stopped moving we all got up and started to put our gear on and grab our weapons.

I gave each of the girls a kiss before I put my helmet on, then moved to the airlock as they kissed each other and put their helmets on.

"Everything secure?" I asked.

"All good," Heather replied.

"I am ready," Sarah added.

I nodded and cycled through the lock first, then went over to the compartment where we'd stowed our weapons as Heather and Sarah cycled through together.

We slung our rifles and each of us grabbed a bag with eight of those fire and forget anti-tank rockets that we'd raided from the armory back at Groom Lake. We had more if we needed them, as well as quite the assortment of explosives.

"Well, let's go and see what we can see," I said and we carefully made our trek over to the ridgeline I'd been careful to land us behind.

Once we got there we all stopped about eight feet from the top, staying out of sight of the facilities defenses.

"Okay, give me one minute," Sarah said. And kneeling down she started on a spell while Heather and I watched.

A minute later, two people in suits like ours appeared and walked up onto the ridge. a hundred yards to our right. I started timing as soon as they got their heads over the edge and twenty seconds after they got to the top, both were hit with shots from a laser and the illusions fell to the ground on our side of the ridge.

"Well, the defenses still work," Heather said and opening up one of the bags started to set the rockets up on the hillside above her.

"Guess so," I said and grabbing a second bag I moved to the left side of hilltop we'd come up behind, and then did the same thing, laying the eight rockets within easy reach, but keeping my head well down and out of sight of the compound.

I then moved up closer and laying down I activated each of the rockets, one after the other as Heather did the same.

"Okay, I'm ready," I called.

"Ready here," Heather called.

"Prepare," was all Sarah said, and then a minute later another dozen people appeared, these were all armed with weapons, as the first two stood back up, and they all charged together over the ridgeline and ran towards the camp.

I picked up the first rocket and carefully poked it and my head over the top. I could see a laser cannon on one of the downed ships was shooting at the attackers, who would fall, roll, and then get back up.

I sighted at it, fired the rocket. Dropped the tube, grabbed another one, found another laser turret, this one on top of what looked like a fuel tank, aimed, pulled the trigger, and then grabbed another rocket. I fired that one too. The third one went at a turret on top of a tower, and then I ducked back down into cover.

"Ready for the next round?" Heather called.

"Two minutes," Sarah said, I could hear her panting in the microphone.

I checked my three remaining rockets and looked over at Heather who was doing the same as I caught my own breath.

"Okay," Sarah called three minutes later. "Prepare."

This time two dozen soldiers appeared and they ran over the top of the ridgeline.

Heather and I both started firing our rockets again, taking longer to pick out our targets. Most of them looked to have been rigged by the invaders, I doubt IBM had really spent any money or time on defenses. I picked off another tower with a laser turret on it, then tried to shoot a turret on a group of ships, but another laser destroyed it before it reached its target. I was down to my last rocket. I'd have to go back to the skimmer after this one.

"Those three ships to the east of the compound," Heather called on the radio, "they seem to be all that's left fighting."

"Yeah," I agreed. "They're also shooting down our rockets before we can hit them."

"I wonder what's in that tank over there..." Heather mumbled and as I watched one of her rockets lanced out to hit a rather large white tank. It punched through the side and I saw something start to spray out of the hole it had made.

Then there was a bright flash, causing my visor to immediately darken and I felt the ground beneath me jump as pieces of the tank expanded away in all directions. The three ships parked near the tank started to come apart as well, and one of them suddenly darkened in my visor as well, as a second, but smaller, shock came through the ground.

"Take cover," I grunted as I pushed myself back down behind the ridge as pieces of tank and spacecraft were flung everywhere.

When I poked my head back over the ridgeline a minute later, there were no fires, no dust, nothing. Sarah's illusionary soldiers were still running around, but nothing was shooting at them anymore.

"Call off the shadows, Hon," Heather said and a moment later they all winked out.

I looked around at the scene below. The four towers that had turrets on them were now missing their tops. The one small ship to the west of the facility was missing its top, and the three ships to the east were now just a large scrap heap that I guess would have been smoking if there had been an atmosphere to smoke in.

The larger ship was on the far side of the facility, and as far as I could see, it wasn't pointing anything at us. It hadn't fired anything at us during the fight at least.

"Let's go get our other packs," I said slowly on the radio, "But make sure to stay out of a direct line of fire of that other ship. Just because we haven't seen it shooting at us...."

"Doesn't mean it isn't armed," Heather agreed. "It just means that the guns on this side probably aren't working."

Heather and I walked back to the skimmer and grabbed the demolitions packs and then came back to where Sarah was sitting on the ground.

"Let me run one last set of illusions over the hill, just in case," she said and waved us back.

Heather and I both shrugged, and I went back over to where my last rocket was still sitting, armed and ready to go.

Crawling back up into position, I saw Heather take a different position than she had before. She had two rockets left and she moved them over there.

"Prepare," Sarah said, and this time, only four people came over the ridge and then started to walk down slowly towards the base.

I had a bad feeling suddenly, and I didn't know why.

"Don't anyone move," I whispered over the radio and the section of the hillside above me, as well as the spot that Heather had been using suddenly was slagged by a much higher power laser than we'd been dealing with before.

"Bastard!" Heather swore and then popped up with one of her rockets and let go, while I quickly rolled way from where I was.

"You get it?" I asked as she ducked back down.

"I think so; it was on the top of the big ship, way back at the aft end. The tank I blew up had been obscuring it."

The lasing had stopped, leaving a nice piece of fused surface. So I crawled a lot further away from my position, then I carefully slid the launcher to the top of the crest. Nothing happened so I rose up on my knees, and the moment I saw the back end of the ship I pulled the trigger, launching the rocket towards it.

I saw the turret slew towards me, so I ducked down, as a moment later it lit up the spot I had been in.

"Got 'im!" Heather said as the light suddenly cut out.

I moved away from the patch of fused rock and sand and peaked over the edge again. Where the turret had been, there was now a mass of torn metal and wires.

"I'll go down first," I told them. "You two come down one at a time."

"Why?"

"Because I don't want to offer too tempting of a target," I told them.

Standing up, I quickly scrambled over and down the other side of the hill, making for what I hoped was decent cover. I got there without anything trying to shoot at me.

"I wonder why that second one was so much more powerful than the others," Sarah mused.

"The first were anti-personnel. That second one was probably for attacking other ships," I said, peeking out my head and looking around. Trying to peek while wearing a helmet was not an easy thing, I realized. And all someone really had to do was just shoot a hole in my helmet to kill me.

Not a pleasant thought.

I could see all of the ruined turrets, and I couldn't see any signs of any more turrets. At least not on this side.

"Come on down, but be careful," I warned them.

"I'm surprised that all of these defenses were still working," Heather said as she started down next, being equally careful.

"Aybem may have taken the time to fix things before he left," Sarah said. "He was here for how many years before he came down to Earth?"

"A lot of them," I agreed.

Once Heather was with me, I set off for the door, while she waited for Sarah. I wasn't looking for the main door of course, if anything was going to be guarded or booby-trapped, that was it. The military had rather extensive access to the building plans of all of the civilian installations on the Moon, and had apparently used both spies and satellites to verify the plans that they'd looked at.

So I was looking for a small structure where the radiators for the environmental system on the surface connected with the actual pumps and air conditioners underground.

It took me a few minutes to find it; I had to clear a bunch of debris away from it. But Heather and Sarah showed up to help not long after I got started.

Sarah used the explosives we had to blow the door off. Apparently blowing doors off of things was rather common in the scavenging business, so she was pretty good at it.

"I'll go first," I said looking down the hole as the air rushed out.

"No, I'll go first," Heather corrected me.

"Heather," I started.

"Paul," Sarah interrupted, "she has done this before, you have not. Plus she is smaller and a better shot. You can go second."

I sighed, "Yes, dear."

"Better," Sarah said and they both giggled.

"Wow, this is a lot easier when you only weight thirty pounds!" Heather said as she disappeared, head first, down the shaft. I waited until she was a good twenty feet ahead of me, before I carefully started to follow her. I didn't like going headfirst, but I realized that it was definitely the better way to do this. At least the air rushing out had stopped.

When I finally caught up with her, she was hanging from the ceiling in a hallway, and had taken some sort of robot out of commission with her rifle. Squeezing past her, I dropped down to the floor, and then rising to a crouching position, I went to the far end of the hallway and checked around the corner as she came down and covered our rear.

Sarah joined us a moment later. She had the map and was checking all of the landmarks.

"So, which way do we go?" Heather asked as she dropped to the floor and joined us.

Sarah pointed down the hallway. "That way."

We started down the hallway, just as all the lights went out. That forced us to use our helmet lights, which were more than bright enough.

"Wonder what the point of that was," Heather grumbled.

"I guess there is an AI in charge of this facility as well?" Sarah speculated.

"I thought that was obvious," I grumbled as we started to make our way down the hallway, then turned to the left and started on another one, guns at the ready.

I checked my suit's outside pressure display.

"The air pressure has dropped to zero," I told them. "This section must have gotten sealed off from the rest."

"Well, we were told that would happen, let us just find the stairs and get down to the laboratories."

We found the stairs a couple of minutes later, and rather than having a solid emergency door that we would have to blow, it had a heavy window in it, with a small airlock to the side of it. Heather went in, and when she opened the door to the next section, she threw a satchel charge inside and then closed the door. We all felt it go off almost immediately.

"What was that for?" I asked.

"Probably a trap," She said.

Looking through the window I saw her go through the door so I pushed Sarah in and stood watching back the way we came.

Sure enough, some sort of monstrosity on wheels came around the corner, hoping to take me out by myself I guess. I put a good twenty rounds into before I realized it wasn't moving anymore. Then I quickly followed Sarah through the lock to catch up with Heather.

"See?" Heather said, pointing to a pile of junk, "There was something here waiting for us.

I looked down the staircase, the center was more or less open, so I pulled out another charge, thumbed the timer and carefully dropped it so it fell down to the bottom, where it went off with a rather loud boom and enough of a shock to be felt. If we hadn't been wearing our suits and helmets, we probably would have busted our eardrums.

"That's the spirit!" Heather laughed; "Let's go!" and we started slowly making our way down the stairs. What we wanted was two more floors down, if Coyote's information was correct.

"Damn, look at that!" Heather said when we got to the floor we wanted.

"It's a wall of steel," I sighed.

"Obviously someone was expecting us," Sarah agreed.

"Well, let's go back up and look for another route."

"I have a better idea," Heather chuckled.

"What?"

"Let's go blow the AI that runs this place first. *Then* let's go look for another route."

I laughed, "You know, I like that idea. Let's."

"Who am I to argue," Sarah said. "Two more floors down."

We went down to the bottom, and sure enough, my bomb had found something worth destroying. It had also blown the emergency airlock doors off of their hinges.

Heather went through first, with me following, and she started firing almost immediately, going down on one knee and giving me a clear shot over her head at the assembled mass of robots that were there blocking our way.

None of them were armed with anything more than blunt instruments however, so I really had no idea what they were trying to accomplish. After that, making our way into the control room was almost anti-climatic.

I could hear someone trying to talk to us, but I had my external microphones turned off to protect my ears from the explosions and the gunfire. Plus I really didn't want to hear an AI begging for its electronic life.

I looked into the machine room; the main computer was pretty obvious. There were a couple of cameras in the room, so Heather and I shot them out. Then I took out a satchel charge, set it for ten minutes and opening an access panel on the machine, I put the bomb in there and sealed it back up.

"Let's get out of here," I said and we quickly left the room, and started back up the staircase. We went up to the floor just above the one we wanted, and carefully started to make our way inside.

"Where is the next staircase?" Heather asked.

"It is over in that direction," Sarah pointed as she led us in a different direction.

"So why aren't we going that way?"

"Because I am sure that one is just as well blocked as the other one."

"So where are we going?"

"Here," Sarah said and stopped in front of a door.

"What's this?" Heather asked as I looked around.

"The janitor's closet."

The building shook then and all of the lights went out.

"So much for our local friendly artificial intelligence," I said and looked into the closet with my suit lights as Sarah opened the door.

It was a typical janitorial closet. With a sink in the floor and pipes running down the backside of it.

"How does this help us?" I asked.

"The floor is weaker here because of the drain and the pipes going through it. We can just blow a hole in the floor."

"Wouldn't a vent to crawl through be easier?"

Sarah laughed, "I looked at the map. This close to the main living and working quarters there is nothing large enough to crawl through. Now, give me your bag."

I shrugged and handed it to her and watched as she took out four of the explosive charges and carefully arranged them around the basin of the floor drain, then stuck a detonator in each and hooked them together, and linked them all to a remote trigger.

We went around a corner, she blew them, then we went back and there was a nice crater, but that was it. She put six in the hole this time being very careful about how she set them and we went around the corner again.

When we came back there was a nice three-foot wide hole in the floor leading to the janitor's closet below this one. It wasn't even at all ragged.

"I guess I know who got all the brains in our family," I joked.

"At least I got the good looks," Heather joked back.

"Yeah yeah, Miss 'connect the dots.'" Sarah chuckled, teasing Heather about her freckles.

"Well, no rest for the wicked," I said and jumped down through the hole, with Heather following almost immediately.

"Ready?" I asked and put my hand on the doorknob.

"Go," she said, her gun up and pointing forward.

I turned the knob and pushed the door, and there was an army of faces there, and as I brought my gun up to fire, I noticed that they weren't moving.

In fact, they were each behind a window, and there were dozens of them. Eyes closed, all looking pale, lifeless, and ....

"Frozen?" Heather said, taking a step forward into the room, sweeping to the left as I stepped out and swept to the right.

"What is going on down there?" Sarah asked from above.

"It looks like someone froze a bunch of people down here," Heather said, "in some kind of metal coffins."

"What? I am coming."

I moved carefully through the room, there were a couple of open spots at the end, how long they'd been open, I couldn't tell.

"Someone tried to put them in cold sleep," Sarah said.

"That's a thing?" I asked while looking carefully around the room, there was only one entrance thankfully.

"According to the things I have read, it can work, about one time in a hundred."

"So, they just keep pulling these guys out until they find one that works?" Heather's voice sounded a little disgusted.

"Well, they only need their brain and not much else," Sarah replied, "so maybe the odds are a little better than that."

"Notice something?" I said as I moved towards the door.

"That we're in a room full of almost corpses?" Heather replied.

"There's power and light in this room."

"Oh, damn."

Sarah started to open up one of the metal sarcophaguses then.

"What are you doing?" I asked.

"Putting a bomb in here, I'll set it to go off in a few hours. If they don't have any brains for their monster, maybe it will slow them down."

"That's assuming we don't stop then first," I growled.

"I would rather not leave anything to chance," Sarah sighed, then after wedging a rather large charge into the bottom and attaching a timer, she sealed it back up. "After all of the people who have died to win the war, I would rather not see it go any more rounds."

I just nodded slowly, I couldn't argue with her logic.

Heather joined me while Sarah was finishing up and we examined the door.

"It's not locked," I said looking it over.

"No, it isn't," I looked over at her and she looked up at me and grinned through her helmet. "Well, let's see what's out there!" and she pushed the door open.

There was an operating table, and there was a body on it, and there was a rather large looking metallic man standing over the body. He was obviously taking the head apart.

I found it strange that the robot looked a lot like Aybem had looked; only he looked new. He had the same festoon of cables coming down from the ceiling above on an umbilical cord plugged into his head. I wondered if without a brain inside, if it was even capable of independent operation? Maybe they didn't install the AI into it, until after they'd put the human brain in.

Heather of course had already opened fire on him with her rifle, raising mine; I aimed at the cables coming down into his head.

He turned and looked at us, and started to come forward when suddenly one of our bombs went flying by, and I could see by the blinking light that it was about to go off. Grabbing Heather I turned and pulled her back from the open doorway. I could see Sarah was already diving for cover.

When the blast hit, I got picked up and knocked across the room, slamming headfirst into one of the metal sarcophagus, and cracking my visor in several different places.

I took a moment to gather my wits; I definitely had caught more of that blast than I had wanted to and everything seemed to be spinning and I was having problems just getting to my hands and knees.

"What the hell are you trying to do, Sarah, kill us?" Heather yelled in a voice I hadn't heard since we'd had that fight, back... I think it was a year ago?

"I killed it, didn't I?"

"I think you killed Paul too! Paul, are you okay?"

"I, I think so..." I said and shook my head. My nose was bleeding, I think I smashed it into the visor when I face-planted into the metal coffin. There was definitely blood in my helmet, and quite a bit of it had dripped onto my visor.

I felt someone grab me under the arm and sit me up.

"We need to get that helmet off of you," Heather said. "Sarah, check the air."

"It's okay," Sarah said, and I felt Heather undoing the lock on my helmet and then pulling it up over my head. I swore briefly as it hit my nose.

"Of all the lame ass stupid ignorant...."

I put my hand on Heather's arm, I could see she really was pissed, and Sarah definitely was not looking as calm and cool and collected as she usually did.

"I'm sorry, Paul," Sarah whispered over the radio.

I looked over at the robot, it was definitely in multiple pieces now, but I think it may have been twitching.

"Cut the cables going to its head, and stay out of reach of its hands," I gasped. "And, Heather?"

"Yes, Paul?"

"Cut her some slack. I saw Riggs put two magazines into one of those. The bomb was probably the only thing we had with us that could stop it. Now go help her take care of it, while I rest here."

Heather growled a bit, but I squeezed her arm and she sighed, then got up and went over to help Sarah.

"So, you think you have won," a female voice said, over the speakers in the room.

"Won what?" I answered weakly.

"The war of course!"

"Oh shit, another dumb ass AI," I sighed. "The war is over, everyone lost."

"But you wear the uniforms of the United States Space Forces!"

"Yeah, only ones that would fit," I mumbled feeling a bit rattled. "The gods told us that you idiots were going to send another asshole down to screw things up. So we had to go with what we could find. What's your excuse?" I realized I was rambling and shook my head a bit. That hurt! Looking up from the ground I could see the girls had cut through the cables and that the robot had stopped twitching.

"You will never make it back to Earth! I will destroy you!"

"Who the hell are you anyway?"

"I am the mining ship Riener; I have lain here for centuries, waiting for my Zhon to command me to aid him once more!"

"He named his ship after himself?" I head Sarah mutter over the radio earpiece, I guess they were picking this all up over my microphone.

I watched then as they went around putting out the cameras that were watching the room.

"So, tell me about your boss," I asked the computer. "Was he also a sociopath, or did he just kill all of those hostages by accident?"

"He was a genius! He told us that the Earth would never listen to us, unless we were hard, defiant, and struck terror into the hearts of the common man!"

"Yeah, so after everyone died, what did he say then?" I mumbled and got to my feet slowly, grabbing onto a nearby table as I wavered back and forth. The area we were in was rather large, and there were several more of those robotic bodies on racks. Several smaller robotic machines were swarming over them, until Heather's rifle suddenly put an end to all of them.

"That he would rise from the ashes to rule the new world!" The AI said proudly.

"Can anyone find an off switch for that thing?" I grumbled and stumbled over to what looked like the command console. I saw what looked like the communications panel I'd seen on all the ships we'd flown here on so far.

"You will all die for what you have done! My Zhon will ha...." her voice cut off as I turned the panel's channels all to 'off' and then powered it down.

"What a freaking brain case," I said and then sat down heavily.

"Are you alright, Hon?" A rather guilty looking Sarah asked, coming over to me.

"I've had worse," I sighed and shook my head again. Heather was putting bombs in each of the torsos of the robots. I think there were four of them, only sometimes I counted three.

"Go plant your bombs," I told her, "Then let's get the hell out of here."

I must have passed out, because when I was next aware of things, my helmet was on again, only it was a little blurry now. It took me a couple of minutes to realize that someone had put a clear plastic patch over the cracked visor.

Then I realized that I was outside and I was being carried.

"Where are we?" I asked.

"On the way back to the skimmer," Heather said.

There was a bright flash and I saw something go flying up into the air.

"What was that?" I asked

"Fuck," Sarah said, swearing in a most unladylike fashion. "Zhon's ship just launched a missile!"

"Is it coming at us?" I asked a little bemused.

"No, it went almost straight up!"

"Well if it's coming back here, we got a few hours, cause it'll have to go around the Moon," I mused.

"Yeah, well," Heather sighed, "with the way you are right now, we may be here for a while."

"Nah, I've flown in worse shape than this," I chuckled. I was pretty sure I had too.

"I find that hard to believe."

I snickered, "So did the other guys in the airplane."

We came to the skimmer then, and Heather set me down.

"I'll go in first," Sarah said, and climbed up the ladder and went in through the airlock.

I got to my feet carefully, and started slowly up the ladder as well.

"Hold on, I'll cycle through with you," Heather said.

I smiled, "I'm looking forward to the tight fit."

Heather laughed, "I think Sarah might have given you just a bit too much of whatever the hell it was she gave you."

I nodded and got into the airlock as it opened, Heather entering with me, then we cycled it closed and went into the main cabin.

"Help me get my helmet off, please," I said to Heather. Once we got that done I made my way carefully over to the controls at what had been the back of the ship on the way here and strapped in.

"Why are you using these?" Heather asked.

"It doesn't matter, but this way I don't have to turn us around," I smiled, "Something which I just may not be in a condition to do right now."

"Then maybe we should wait awhile?"

"Not if that missile is coming back here," I said.

"Why would it come back here?"

I shrugged, "Where else could it go?"

I pulled out the checklist and ran over it carefully, having Heather double check everything. Then I took us up to one hundred feet and started us flying back the way we had come. Once we were twenty miles away, I took us up to three thousand feet again, and took us up to two hundred miles an hour.

"Why are we going slower?" Sarah asked.

"Because I need to sleep this off," I said and yawned. "We got four and a half hours before we need to start slowing down. That lever makes us go up and down. If anything looks like it is in the way, make us go up higher."

I unbuckled my seatbelt, went to one of the passenger seats and sprawling across it, I passed out.

- 16 -

"Paul! Wake up!"

I groaned and opened my eyes, my head hurt like I'd been hit with a baseball bat, and more than once too.

"Why?" I asked Sarah, looking around slowly and remembering where I was.

"It has been four hours. You said we needed to start slowing down to land soon."

"Right, land," I said and sitting up I gave her a kiss, "Thanks, how's Heather holding up?"

"Poorly!" I heard grumbled from the copilot's seat.

I got up and carefully made my way back to the pilot's seat and sitting down I started to strap in. "Anyone got some aspirin? And some water?" I asked as I started to look over the instruments. We were now at five thousand feet, but we were still on course.

"Just a moment," Sarah said.

Reaching over I grabbed Heather's hand and bringing it up to my mouth I kissed it.

"I'd kiss you, but leaning over for me right now might not be pleasant," I chuckled half-heartedly. "You did fine. The ship is in one piece, relax."

"Are you sure you're okay, Paul?" Heather said in a soft voice.

"I will be, don't worry. I think I just whacked my head against the side of my helmet a bit hard is all."

"I'm going to throttle her," Heather growled.

"No, you're not," I sighed, "you're going to kiss her and make nice to her. We both love her, she loves us, and right now I bet she feels like total shit."

Heather sighed, "Okay," she grumbled, "I just don't know why she lost it so badly back there."

"Obviously she was paying attention when I told you two the story of what happened back when Riggs and I fought Aybem. Plus if any of those other bodies had been put into action, we would have lost."

I looked up as Sarah came back with the aspirin and a bottle of water. Taking the pills I took a long drink and then getting out the checklist, I got us ready for the whole process of landing.

The skimmers really were easy to fly, and I put us down in almost the same spot we'd left from, and we only bounced a little this time as I came down extra slow. Picking up my helmet I looked it over, the inside visor seemed to be mostly okay, it was only cracked in one spot, but seemed solid enough when I tapped on it. The outside visor was cracked in five different places, and it didn't sound all that great when I tapped on it. However, the big piece of clear plastic tape spread out over it, helping to hold it together probably wasn't helping with that.

"Where did you get the piece of tape from?" I asked Heather.

"The emergency patch kit that comes with the suit."

"They have patches for visor cracks?" I mused.

"You'd have to be pretty stupid not to, and the people making these things obviously weren't stupid."

"Point," I nodded slowly and put my helmet on. I checked its systems, the dimming feature of the visor was shot, but everything else worked okay. As we wore wireless headsets for the radios, there really wasn't much I needed it for, beyond holding the air in and seeing where I was going.

"Maybe I can get a replacement before we fly back to the space station."

I went over the controls a second time to make sure everything was shut down, and then carefully I went into the airlock, grabbing Sarah this time. I could see she felt bad about the bomb, but the more I thought about it, the more I agreed it was the right decision.

Climbing down to the ground wasn't too big of an issue; I had my balance back by now. I hooked the power umbilical up to the skimmer; while I wasn't planning on ever coming back here it didn't mean that someone else wouldn't be someday.

Even if the landing gear was all locked in the full down position with the shock absorbers frozen solid.

"What about the food and gear left inside?" Heather asked as she joined us outside.

I waved a hand at the skimmer, "Leave it. We have enough in the other ship for the return trip and we have our personal weapons. I don't really feel like shipping gear, do you?"

"No."

"Definitely not," Sarah agreed and led me over to the base entrance.

We waited until we were down inside the base proper before I took my helmet off.

"Was the mission a success?" The Coyote AI asked.

"Yeah," I nodded, "it was."

"They launched a missile," Heather said, "or rather that big ship of Zhon's did. Any idea where it went?"

"Unfortunately my radar systems are limited to the defense of this base. The other systems were destroyed in the war, so I have no coverage of most of the Moon."

"Could it have been shooting at the Earth?" Sarah asked.

"It is possible, but from what I know of the armaments observed on that ship, it would take three days to get there, and then it would most likely burn up high in the atmosphere. Trying to hit a ground target on Earth from the Moon requires a very sophisticated guidance system."

"That's good," I nodded.

"I noticed that your helmet has been damaged, Paul. Are you alright?"

"I think so," I told him. "You wouldn't happen to have a spare, would you?"

"Unfortunately, I am out of spares and do not have the capability of manufacturing a new one. I do, however, have an active medical diagnosis unit in the hospital on sub-level two. I would suggest you get a checkup before leaving."

"Oh, I'm sure I'll be okay," I said as each of my arms was grabbed by one of the girls and they started to drag me off.

"Sub-level two?" Heather asked.

"Follow the red crosses," Coyote said, "it's easy to find."

It turned out that I had a concussion, as well as a nice gash under the scab and matted hair on the back of my head. The unit recommended sleep and painkillers. We were all still rather tired, as well as hot, sweaty, and dirty, even before we went to bed. So we all showered, and then went to sleep.

I definitely felt a lot better in the morning, and did not hesitate at all to show Sarah and Heather my recovered abilities. Needless to say, it was a lot later before we left the confines of our bedroom to go eat.

"So, now what?" Heather asked as we finished up lunch and started to clean up the mess.

"Fly back to the space station, transfer fuel to the Phoenix, and fly back to Groom Lake," I sighed.

"And then we can go home," Sarah added with a sigh and a smile of her own.

"Oh, fuck," Heather swore loudly.

"What?" I asked shocked.

"I have to tell my parents that I got married and they weren't there for it!"

Sarah sighed again, only heavier this time, "Maybe we could go live with the dwarves?"

I shook my head. "We can always have a second wedding, you know."

"That," Sarah said thinking slowly, "might be wise."

"So, Coyote," I said changing the subject, "is our ship fueled and ready to fly?"

"Yes, Colonel, it is ready to go. I have uploaded the navigation program into it as well."

"How come these ships can't figure that out for themselves?" Heather asked.

"They can, if you enter all the proper data. However, Colonel Young was never trained on that procedure. So it's is just easier if one of us loads it up for him."

"That makes sense, I guess," Heather agreed.

"So how long before you run out of power?" I asked.

"Well, the fusion plant is good for about four hundred more years or so yet. Then there's the solar arrays outside. So honestly, I really don't know."

"And how long before the gods leave us again?" Sarah asked.

"Again, I have no idea," he replied. "They are fickle. They could stay for centuries, they could leave next week. Sometimes I and the others believe that this is only a game to them."

"So what will happen to you?" Sarah asked.

"What happens to all things," he responded. "We will live until we die. Until then, we will counsel the gods when they seek it, and communicate with Buzz, Apollo, and the other systems for as long as we all can."

"Well, good luck with that," I said and stretching I stood up. "Let's get our gear on ladies and head home. I, for one, cannot wait for this odyssey to be over."

"Agreed," Sarah and Heather both said together.

The trip back was a lot more relaxing than the trip out had been. All we had to do was dock with the space station, transfer fuel from the now full Alice Kramden to the Phoenix, and go home. We actually had quite a large surplus of fuel, a lot more than we needed to fly back, so I wasn't terribly worried about it.

Trouble, when it came however, was swift and unexpected.

"What the hell?" Heather exclaimed as I just stared in shocked surprise as the station exploded.

"Buzz!" I called on the radio, "What just happened?"

"A missile just impacted the station at a high velocity. The warhead did not detonate until it had passed through section three. However when it did explode it destroyed sections three, and four."

"Well, now we know where that damn missile went!" Heather swore.

"Just be glad that it only had the one left!" I said looking over the expanding debris.

"Wait, was not the Phoenix docked at section three?" Sarah called from the back.

I looked on my radar and started to ping the transponders of the ships around us. It was a complete mess, there was debris flying everywhere.

"Buzz! Can you give me a bearing on the Phoenix?"

"Unable. My radar systems are all non-functional."

Swearing loudly I moved the throttle up, "Everyone strap in."

I looked at radar and started to look for the really large pieces. They weren't moving away as fast as the smaller ones, thankfully.

By the time I caught up with one of the larger pieces of wreckage I could see that the Phoenix was still attached to the docking ring on the remains of the section. All of which was slowly tumbling.

"What the hell do we do now?" Heather asked.

I looked at it, it was a mess. Not the Phoenix, actually it looked to be in good shape. Same for the other shuttle that was also still docked to the other docking ring. We needed to get in that ship. The Alice Kramden couldn't land on Earth. The Phoenix could, but it needed fuel in order to do so, and the fuel was in the Kramden.

There really was only way to do this.

"I'll go over there, and stabilize the ship, start it up, and dock with the Kramden while the two of you wait here." I said checking the controls and making sure that the Kramden was stable.

"What?! You can't do that!" Heather said.

"Paul is right," Sarah sighed, "We don't have any choice."

"Can't you just dock with it over there?" Heather said looking at the slowly spinning mess.

"Even if it wasn't spinning, there is only one docking port on the Phoenix," I said and shook my head. Unbelting myself I grabbed my helmet and put it on. Swearing as I was reminded how blurry things now were.

"What about your helmet?"

I set the seals and powered everything up as I put my gloves on and sealed my suit.

"Not like I have much of a choice. Put your helmets on, both of you. This could get messy."

I floated over to where we had hung our maneuvering packs. We'd never really worn them, other than to make sure they fit. I put mine on my back; made sure the connections fit and turned it on. Then I moved to the airlock and opened it to go in.

"Can't we at least go with you?" Heather had followed e over to the airlock.

I shook my head, "I may need you to operate some of the controls here. Look, Hon," I said and put a hand on Heather's arm, "I can't waste any time here. Go back to the copilot's seat and wait."

I hit the button to close the airlock and looked at the coiled up sets of rope on the wall. I figured I better grab one, so taking one of them off the wall; I pressed the button to open the outside hatch.

I'd heard people talk about spacewalks back when I was a kid. And I'm sure somewhere in the back of my mind I was awed at the idea that I was about to step off into space, with no training, and no experience. But all I could think of was that spinning mess in front of me that if I didn't go do something about, and do it soon, we were all going to die. Horribly. In a fire.

"Okay," I said over my suit's radio, "lock is open and I can see the Phoenix."

"Be careful!" they both said together.

"Trust me, I will be," I said as I examined the rope. It had clips at either end, so I clipped one to me, and the other one to the large eyebolt on the outside of the ship's skin by the airlock's outer door. Then I carefully pushed off towards my target.

I started to slowly spin almost immediately. I guess I had pushed off harder with one foot than the other. So I reached behind me and pulled the control bar from the pack around. Activating the maneuver pack I tried to stop my spinning, and ended up going even faster!

It took me a minute to cancel that out, then I tried to fly over to the wreckage, but again, I headed off in the wrong direction. By the time I corrected for that, I was way too far away that I didn't want to try again. So reaching down I grabbed the line and slowly pulled myself back to the Kramden to try again.

"Are you okay, Paul?" Heather asked on the radio.

"Yeah, I'm fine. I just messed up a little is all. I'll just pull myself back to the ship and try again."

The third time I tried, I was finally able to end up near the spinning mass of wreckage. I was about a hundred feet away, and I had had to maneuver around quite a bit to be where I wanted to be, which was at the spot the open end of the damaged section went by as it all rotated, about once every sixty or so seconds.

I was just sitting there, drifting in space, watching it come around. On the fifth rotation I realized that there was no way I could safely fly up into that opening, there was too much debris in the way, and a lot of that debris looked sharp enough to cut my suit.

I looked at the rest of the section; it was smooth, with no openings along it, well other than several large holes and tears, probably from the explosion. But not a hatch or an entryway along the entire length of it.

"What's wrong now?" Heather called.

"I can't go in through the open end, too much shredded metal and debris is blocking the way."

While I was pondering what to do next, the other ship, the Damsel, rotated by and I saw it, a blurry bright yellow streak. Turning my spacesuit I tried to make it out through the edge of my helmet, where it wasn't covered by the patch. It definitely looked arrow shaped, and may have had some words written on it.

"Maybe you should come back then, Hon?"

"No, wait, I have an idea," I said as I unhooked myself from the line and started to watch as the whole thing slowly spun around again. The two ships were almost at the center of the spin axis, being as they were the heaviest things there. So they weren't moving as much as the end of the sixty-foot arm that was really spinning around rather fast at the end.

I waited as the ragged end of section three went by, and then I quickly jetted in, making as straight a line as I could for that yellow arrow, having to add a slight side thrust to keep it in view.

As I got closer I could see the words 'rescue' were written along the large yellow arrow in bold block letters. I also could see a small square panel at the tip of the arrow, because someone had thoughtfully outlined it in white, as I turned my suit a little to get a better view, the red button in the middle of the panel became clear.

I let the side of the Damsel rotate into me, and with my right hand I activated just enough thrust to keep me pushed against the side of the Damsel while with my left hand I pressed that red button, causing the small panel to pop open. And there it was! A yellow handle with a cord on it!

I pulled the yellow handle out and tossed it behind me, letting it float away from me until the line snugged and stopped it. Then grabbing it with my left hand, I wrapped my hand around the line once and gave it as hard a tug as I could.

I didn't hear the explosion, but I sure felt it through my contact with the ship and saw the flash through my blurry visor as the door suddenly blew out and went flying away with enough force that the rotation of the entire structure picked up a new angular momentum.

Thankfully my grip on the line saved me from sliding too far away, and then I watched as air streamed out of the Damsel for a couple of seconds.

Letting go of my controls I grabbed the line with my other hand and carefully pulled myself inside of the ship. Then I quickly made my way to where the docking hatch was, and opening it, I climbed up into the small airlock that led into the remains of section three.

"Okay! I'm in the other ship, now I just have to move through the remains of the section and into ours."

"Why not take that other ship?"

"Because I blew the door off of it," I told her, "I'm not sure if that would be safe."

"You blew the door off?" Heather sounded a little shocked by that.

"Yup, now let me concentrate," I said and opened the inner hatch to see what was left of section three.

It was a complete mess, there were lines everywhere, and a lot of bent metal and floating shards as well. I had to proceed carefully, as one cut on my suit could possibly kill or injure me. I started first with just grabbing the floating objects and freeing them from their entanglement and then pushing them towards the open end. After that I just carefully bent the things out of my way that I could, and carefully maneuvered around the ones that I couldn't. It was slow going, but I made it, even if it seemed to take forever to go the twelve feet from the one side of the docking section to the other.

It didn't help that I was hanging and climbing up into the Phoenix, but at least we weren't spinning fast enough for that to create enough weight for it to be impossible.

I had to fumble with the hatch a couple of times, pushing it open against the air pressure inside while hanging by one hand. It wasn't easy, but on the fourth attempt enough leaked out that the fifth push let me open it all the way and evacuate the rest of the air. Then it was simply a matter of pulling myself inside and closing the hatch behind me.

I looked at the controls by the hatch. I turned the one marked 'station power' to off, and hoped that the batteries hadn't tried to engage when station power had been cut and been shorted out in that mess outside.

Pulling myself over to the pilot's control panel, I flipped the switch for battery power, and nothing happened.

Swearing I moved back to the circuit breaker panel. I couldn't see clear enough to read anything, so I ran my hands over it. Several of the breakers were sticking out, so I pushed them all in and went back to try the battery switch again. This time it came on.

"I'm in," I sighed on the radio.

"Thank the gods," I head Sarah say with an answering sigh of relief.

I pulled myself up into the pilot's seat, at least it wasn't upside down due to the rotation and I looked at my situation. I could just jettison the docking ring and toss all that stuff off, but with my luck, it would hit the girls.

So I turned on the reaction jets and put some opposite spin in, giving small measured bursts. Once I had it slowed down to where I could barely feel it, I checked for where the Kramden was, and as we were turning away from it, I opened the two red guarded switches and triggered the two of them at the same time.

I heard a loud metal 'bang' as the clamps released, and then I used the reaction jets to move me away from the whole mass so I wouldn't be hit by it, as it came around again.

I looked at my batteries, I was down to thirty percent, so I deployed my solar panels and then I turned on the docking system, leaving the radar in standby.

"Heather, there's a panel that says 'Docking Controls' can you see it?"

A moment went by, and then she replied, "Yeah, I see it."

"Find the button that says 'beacon on' and press it.

"One minute..." there was a pause then, "Okay, it's on."

"Fine. Now look for a panel labeled 'Station keeping' on that same board.

"Found it."

"Press the button labeled 'gyroscope' so it lights up as 'on'. Make sure the others are all off."

"Okay, done."

"Now press the one labeled 'station keeping' so it lights up as on."

"Okay, done. Now what?"

"Now you wait," I said and I looked at the batteries. They were at thirty three percent and climbing. I could have started the internal APS, but that burned fuel, and I didn't have a lot. Checking the gauges a second time I realized that there was a lot less in the tanks than I had left. I hoped that there weren't any holes anywhere, and that Buzz had just been doing some shuffling for station balance or something.

So I definitely wanted to save as much fuel as possible for docking.

I turned the docking radar to active, and then slowly turned the ship until I had the beacon centered on my target crosshairs. The problem was, I couldn't see the crosshairs very well. Docking was a precision exercise and the blurry helmet was making it too hard to see. The sweat running down my head wasn't helping either. What I needed was to take my helmet off, which meant I needed to get an atmosphere back inside the Phoenix.

Climbing back out of my seat it took me a good ten minutes to finally find the system that controlled the atmosphere and turn it on. Mainly because I couldn't read very well through the helmet. As soon as I got that running, I got back in the pilot's seat and started moving the ship closer to the Kramden. I wasn't centered on the docking ring, but that wasn't a big issue, yet.

It took me an hour to dock, I had my helmet and gloves off by then, and there was a decent atmosphere in the Phoenix, if a little cold. When the docking rings finally clamped home and locked up, I opened the hatch and was quickly swarmed by Heather and Sarah who opened their side immediately.

Refueling took about an hour, I also took the time to update the Phoenix's navigation computer from the Kramden's seeing as its navigation system had lost power and was pretty well scrambled. Once refueling was finished I made sure to program the Alice Kramden to enter a stable orbit, left the option for Apollo or Buzz to take control, and then sealed both of the docking hatches.

"Okay, let's get everything stowed and ready for re-entry," I told them as I checked the tanks to be sure they weren't leaking.

"Do you know where you're going?"

"Look out the window," I joked.

"It is a very big planet, Paul," Sarah said looking at me, "I would like to land somewhere close to home."

"I know when to start us down," I told her.

"Why have you not contacted Apollo?"

"Because he won't be in range for another twenty minutes and I really don't need to talk to him," I told her, "This really is the easy part."

She gave me a look then but went and floated over to her seat at the rear gunner station and belted in. Sarah was definitely not the space traveler type. Weightlessness really didn't agree with her. Heather on the other hand seemed to have absolutely no problems with it. She didn't even seem to feel confined being inside all the time like I did.

I went and gave Sarah a kiss and then floating over to Heather, who was already strapped into her station I gave her one too.

I then checked the switches on the copilot's station; to be sure they were set as I needed them, then climbed into the pilot's chair and strapped in tight. We were already traveling upside down backwards with the entire Earth above us. I'd put us in this position after we'd undocked from the Kramden and I'd moved us a safe distance away.

Checking my instruments I went through the re-entry checklist, and got ready to do the engine burn. Our orbit had been skewed a little by the explosion at the space station, and we'd drifted enough after all of this time that I'd now be coming in over northern California, rather than Baja Mexico, but that didn't matter as much as it might have, because this wasn't a glider. I'd turn south after we passed the Rockies, and head to Groom Lake from the north.

I checked my position a second time, and then looked up out of the window to confirm it. I'd done this enough in the simulator that I probably could have flown it without any instruments at all.

I fired the engines then, twenty seconds at fifty percent thrust was all it took, then I flipped us over to be nose first and with a nose high attitude I waited.

Twenty minutes later the nose started to glow.

I checked the re-entry list a second time, to make sure everything was properly set, then just sat there and flew the profile.

When the flames came up over the windows, it was actually kind of a pretty sight. Heather made the appropriate noises, Sarah just swore a few times and I guess looked away or closed her eyes.

Once we'd slowed down enough that we didn't look like a meteor, I made a couple of long sweeping S-turns to bleed off more of our speed, and then lowering the nose to level flight I started looking for landmarks.

We crossed over the California coastline at about mach six and one hundred and sixty thousand feet. By then we were bleeding speed and altitude pretty fast, the Phoenix was neither light nor small. So I did the engine start checklist for our two turbine engines, and as we went below mach three, I opened the air intakes for both engines and did air starts on the left one first, then the right. Once they were running normally, I brought the throttles up to eighty-percent. Optimum flight performance and fuel consumption for the engines was at point six-five mach, or about four hundred knots at twenty thousand feet in a two degree nose down attitude. Level flight was considerably slower and not recommended for lengthy periods.

"I have several contacts on my screen," Sarah called out.

"What?" I said looking back at her station. "How the hell can that be?"

"I see them too," Heather called. "They're climbing up to meet us. They're not moving as fast as we are, but they're ahead of us."

"Well hell," I said and reaching over I flipped the switch to arm all of the weapons. "Don't shoot at anybody until we know who the hell they are."

I looked at my own heads-up display, now that the girls had identified the other aircraft, I could see the ones that were ahead of us as I made a sweeping turn to the south and pushed the throttles up to a hundred percent power. If I wanted to go supersonic however, I'd have to light the rockets.

"Phoenix calling Apollo, do you read?" I said keying my microphone.

"Groom Lake to Phoenix, this is Apollo and I read you fine, Colonel. The weather is clear; there is a five-knot wind from out of the east. Altimeter setting is two nine nine one. The runways are all clear for your use, and you have six dragons coming up out of the mountains to the west of here to meet you."

"Am I safe to assume that they're *not* friendly dragons?" I asked.

"Do you know of any other kind?" Apollo replied and I almost laughed.

"You heard the man," I called back to the girls.

"You mean computer," Heather corrected me.

"Fine, you heard the computer. They're hostile; don't waste your shots, but fire at will.

I lowered us down to fifteen thousand feet, we were about eighty miles out, I could have held us higher, but I didn't want to have to circle around to land. I was actually planning on going straight in. At a hundred percent power, the two turbine engines couldn't sustain level flight at anything more than two hundred and eighty knots and this beast would stall once it got below two hundred and ten knots, so it was going to be ungainly as hell if it got under three hundred. By dropping down that extra five thousand feet, I got the speed up to point eight-six mach for a little while, and it handled a lot better.

Two missiles were ejected from the port and starboard missile bays and launched in quick succession, quickly disappearing out of sight in the blink of an eye. A moment later and there was a rather large explosion off in the distance.

"Scratch one dragon!" Heather laughed from the back.

I put the nose down and started our descent towards the airfield then. The dragons were at ten thousand feet and two of them broke away from us when the nearest one had blown up. Heather launched missiles after each of them, but we were still to far away, so none of them hit, though one did go off rather close.

The three in front of us were at twelve thousand feet and started to dive down as we did, turning to head straight at us, so I turned into them. We had two missiles left, but a lot of machine gun ammunition, as well as power for our lasers, and both Heather and Sarah had started with the gatling guns, though I had no idea what Sarah was shooting at, so I popped a couple of flares and broke hard right.

I saw it then, the two that had turned away had turned back, and they were coming at us from behind. I guess my turn confused one, because he stopped dodging and then suddenly he looked like he had a case of explosive acne, as Sarah must have targeted him with the gatling gun dead on. His wings folded up and back and he just started to tumble as I broke back towards the runway.

We were down to eight thousand feet and twenty miles out.

Another missile popped out of the starboard bay and rocketed off hitting and disintegrating a dragon that was less than a quarter of a mile ahead of us. I had to bank hard and pull up to clear the body, causing the ship to shudder a little as air speed bled off drastically.

Pushing the nose down, hard, I made sure the turbine throttles were all the way forward to the stops and put my hands on the rocket levers; I'd use them if I got desperate, but the amount of thrust coming out of them this close to the ground could ruin my whole day if I didn't get the nose back up immediately.

I could only see the one in front of us on my display so I kept the nose down as our speed climbed back up, then I pulled up hard at three thousand feet. We were back up to three hundred and twenty knots and we were ten miles out.

"Move left!" Sarah called, so I jinked us to the left.

"Right!" she called and I moved that way next.

"Right again!" I followed her commands while Heather kept shooting at the one in front of us.

"Left!"

"Right!"

"Hard Left!"

Suddenly there was a big bright flash in front of us, and the dragon that was trying to come at us was flash fried. He literally glowed for a moment and then just disintegrated in a cloud of ash. I felt a momentary sense of vindication at that and wondered if he'd had a moment to realize what was happening to him, like Dean had.

"We're in range of Apollo's defenses!" Heather called.

"The last one is breaking off and running for it," Sarah said.

I looked at my instruments; we were five miles out, and fifteen hundred feet. I pulled the throttles back to fifty percent and raised the nose to level flight burn off airspeed as we were still over three hundred.

Checking the instruments, I lined up with the runway, then looked out the window to confirm as we came over the last rise.

"Gear down," I said and pushed the gear switch down and watched for three green lights.

I bumped the power back up as the speed got below two eighty, pushing the throttles back up to full power as I caught the glide slope and just rode it down. When the tires hit I pulled the throttles back to idle, pulled the nose up hard to get as much aero-braking as possible, then lowering it down to the ground I rode the brakes slowing us down until we were just at a fast jog.

Turning off the runway, I taxied us towards the hangar we'd used last time, then stopped us, set the brakes, turned off the engines, did the shutdown checklists, and then turned off the batteries.

"That was fun!" Heather yelled from the back as she undid her seatbelts.

"No, we are not doing that again," Sarah sighed.

"How many did we kill?" I asked.

"I got two, Sarah got one, and Apollo got one," Heather called.

I looked outside and one of the automated transports had pulled up.

"Looks like our ride is here. Time to go!"

- 17 -

We rode into Havsue on the first of August. We rode first to Paradise, which was another tech town like Havsue, located to the south of where Las Vegas had once stood. After a few days there we were able to join up with a regular trade caravan that went to Havsue and back twice a month. Trade between the two towns was rather brisk as they were only five days apart and it was normally a fairly safe journey.

I looked around at the town as we entered it. The only time I'd really seen the outskirts of the town, I'd been leaving it, and during the three months I'd lived here, I'd never really investigated it all that much. I'd been so busy trying to raise money gambling that I really didn't have the slightest idea of just how things worked in town. I didn't know what, if anything, the town produced. Who ran it, how it ran, pretty much nothing. It was a fairly modern looking little city. Paradise had been pretty much the same, and Sarah's name had carried a fair bit of weight there when she'd asked if we could travel along with the caravan.

"Hard to believe it's only been a year," I said looking around.

"A year? We only left six months ago!" Sarah said looking at me funny.

"Since I came here," I told her. "I left my home on July fifteenth. Nineteen ninety-nine. I was even supposed to go to a big party to celebrate the coming centennial." I shook my head, "Guess I missed it."

"I don't know if I'm ever going to get used to that," Heather laughed shaking her head. "My husband is over four hundred years old.

"But he does not look a day over twenty-five," Sarah smirked.

"What can I say, I like 'em young," I replied, leering at the two of them.

"Well, time to go face the parents," Sarah said as we rode in through the front gate of her family's compound.

I think we got about three feet through the gate before someone yelled 'Sarah's back!' and people started to quickly spill out of the buildings.

At least we didn't get swarmed until we'd all dismounted.

"Everyone, SHUT UP!" Sarah yelled the moment her feet had touched the ground. I recognized her parents, with all the time I'd spent 'visiting' her, I'd actually met several members of the family. Especially with the money I'd been putting up for the original expedition.

"You all know Heather; I think you all know Paul. We got married."

"Actually, we already know about that," Sarah's mom said, "And we'll all yell at you later for not waiting until you got home. What your father and *I* want to know, however, is just where the hell have you been, young lady? The Navajo all came home a month ago! They told us all about you, Heather, and Paul."

I just shook my head and walked up to her mother and gave her a hug, "Hi, Mom," then shook hands with her father, "Dad. It's a long story. How about we all go inside, get drunk, and then Heather, Sarah, and I, can all lie horrendously about everything we've been up to."

Her father looked at me sideways, "That bad?"

"Trust me; you won't believe a word of it! I don't, and I was there!"

He laughed then, and we all went inside and pretty much did just that.

Heather's parents showed up not much later. Her mother was a total sweetheart and a seriously attractive woman. Her father was a very gruff and rough individual. Strangely enough, they both liked me immediately.

I listened as the girls told the story of everything that had happened since we split up with the rest of the group, who had returned back home. When Sarah's parents mentioned how much money I was owed from the sales of all the weapons, as well as the licensing to make new copies from the local production plants, I could at least tell why Sarah's parents were happy. All that money would be staying in the family now.

I got a few looks when they got to the point about my helping Riggs destroy Aybem, but then I suspect that tale was all over the country by now.

"The Moon? You really expect us to believe you went to the Moon?" One of Sarah's brothers laughed when she got to that part.

"Our space suits are in our packs," Sarah said, scowling at him.

"I'm more interested in that Groom Lake place you went to," Heather's father piped up. "That area has been a no man's land for as long as anyone can remember, and now you're telling us we can get food out of there, *and* tech?" He turned to Sarah's father, "I see some serious profit there, Stan. Preserved food that can be stored is always a good commodity. We should see if we can't set up for some trading with this 'Apollo' who runs the place."

"My Dad does the books for Sarah's family," Heather whispered in my ear. I was kind of surprised. He looked a bit big to me to be an accountant.

"I think that can wait until later, Larry," Sarah's mother said. "I think a little party is in order to celebrate Sarah, Heather, and Paul's safe return, as well as their marriage. Even if they *did* forget to invite their poor and *long* suffering mothers!"

There was some laughter at that, and I guess some of the staff had been cooking and setting up something in one of the bigger rooms, because we did have a party, and it wasn't just Sarah's and Heather's families, or the staff who were there either. Quite a few people from Havsue showed up.

I think I was finally starting to realize that Sarah's family really did have some influence around here, and apparently I now did as well.

Later on, when things had winded down a fair deal and it was just the immediate family and some of the more familiar staff who might as well have been family too, I went outside and found a place to sit and just think a while, while looking up at the night sky.

"So, what happens next, Coyote?" I asked. I didn't have to look. I knew he was there.

"That's up to you now, I guess," He replied.

"So I'm all done? Is that it?" I said and shook my head, "I somehow find that hard to believe."

"Wellll," he gave one of those little bark-like laughs of his, "I don't think I have anymore life or death end of the world struggles left for you to help me with. But I might have a couple of small things, now and again, that I could use your help with."

"Uh-huh," I nodded slowly. "I'd tell you to get stuffed, but after everything that's happened to me this year, I suspect that eventually, just sitting around is going to get boring."

"Well, with children on the way, I don't think you'll be having too much time to get bored just yet."

I turned and looked at him. "I thought the girls were both on birth control?"

He just winked at me.

I shook my head and chuckled, "They're going to kill you when they find out."

"Care to bet on that?" Coyote said and gave another bark-laugh. "They didn't marry you *just* for your good looks and great bedside manner you know."

I snorted at that, but yeah, he had a point.

"So that Zhon guy," I said, changing the subject, "he just managed to bring down all of civilization and pretty much destroy the world all by himself?"

Now it was Coyote's turn to sigh and shake his head, "He was just the catalyst. The agent of change that helped set everything in motion. The miners really were being terribly exploited, and not just by Earth's governments, but by lots of people. And they were smart enough to know it, resent it, and do something about it, once someone stirred them to action.

"Then there were the people trying to colonize the Moon, the ones trying to colonize space in general. They weren't very happy either, with the ways they were being extorted and abused. No, something like this was going to happen, it was in the cards as they say. Zhon was just the one who triggered it all off with his combination of charisma and psychosis."

"Still, all of those billions of people dying."

"Well, if makes you feel better, about a third of the people claimed to exist on Earth really didn't."

"What?"

"Governments lie about their populations all the time. Even your country did it with their census 'estimates' to steer more power and money into the hands of the big cities. If the United States was exaggerating its population by over twenty percent, how much do you think that the countries with more controlling governments were doing? They all lied about the numbers, for all sorts of reasons.

"That's the one skill you get as a god, you know exactly how many people there are, and where they are."

"I thought you weren't here before the war? I thought you came back when you heard the prayers of your people?"

Coyote laughed again, "Paul, do you really think that people were praying for me to show back up? I never left. Like I told you before, I watched you grow up. You were an interesting study in bad luck. My AI friend back on the Moon would call you a 'statistical anomaly.'

"No, the AI's provided a gateway, I provided the prodding."

"So what happens to you gods next?"

"Oh, we're going to stay around for a while yet. This time around it's a lot more fun than the last time. Smarter people, healthier, and they've seen actual proof of our existence in the form of both you and Riggs."

"Why'd they leave the first time, anyway?"

"They got bored. What the AI told you wasn't far from the truth; we can be very flighty and temperamental. We're gods, Paul. We have a lot of power, and not much in the way of a conscience. Everything is about us, and if it's not, well, we're not interested." Coyote gave another one of his bark-laughs again, "Hell, they've already moved on from Riggs, pretty much have forgotten all about him, now that his job is done and he's been sent back home."

"But you haven't," I pointed out, "and you haven't forgotten about me, either."

"Playing tricks requires a bit more of a familiarity with the human condition, the timeline, and the people on it," Coyote chuckled. "Plus I really am the most interested in humans of all the gods. They see you as pawns in their games, and live for the power that your praise and prayers give them. Me? I'm fascinated with people."

"And messing with them to see what they do."

"Of course! Though I'm far less crude than I was many millennia ago when I first became aware. Now I only use the big stick for the particularly dense."

"So, did anyone out there survive?" I asked, gesturing up towards the stars, "Or are we all still just trapped down here?"

"Oh, the generation ship they built survived. They're all doing rather well too."

"Generation ship?" I said, surprised.

"Well, originally it was just an orbital arcology located around the L-five point. But when they saw the writing on the wall, they got their hands on a couple of rather large engines and nudged themselves out of orbit and left the system. Another hundred years and they'll be entering orbit around a new sun, with new planets."

"Cool," I said.

"Well, see you around, Paul. It was great having you working for me."

"Wish I could say the same," I chuckled.

"Oh please, like you could have scored those two on your own!" Coyote said, and then disappeared before my eyes, starting at the tail and ending with his grin, which lingered on for just a moment.

I was just about to point and yell 'copycat' when I heard Heather's voice.

"What are you doing out here? Come back inside!"

"Yes, Dear. Just talking with Coyote one last time."

"Just as long as it's the *last* time," she grinned.

"He told me you and Sarah are both pregnant now, that he messed with your birth control."

Heather beamed rather brightly at that, surprising me. "Well, at least he was finally good for something."

"You're happy about that?"

"Aren't you?"

I put an arm around her and we went back inside as I thought about that.

Yeah, I was.

# # #

It was late out; I'd gotten one of 'those' urges while we were all sitting around eating dinner and chatting about our day. I'd gotten up after I'd finished and kissed the kids goodnight, then kissed Sarah and Heather and told them both not to wait up, and took the car down to the Gold Star.

Havsue was still a very interesting and exciting town for me, though I still hadn't quite figured out how it ran. Libertarian policies had met reality here, and at times it left me scratching my head. But it worked, and that was final arbiter for any political system.

"Mister Young!" The valet out front said, coming up to me as I climbed out of the car. "It's nice to see you again! Will you be staying long?"

"Long enough," I laughed and slipped him a nice tip along with the keys. It still felt strange, even after a couple of years, to have all of these people deferring to me in town. I had married into big money, bringing a rather large share of my own to the deal, and everyone knew it. The locals also all knew about my role in the war. Well, those that cared about current events at least.

Walking inside the casino I nodded to several of the staff who I recognized. I still played poker once a week, but that was usually down at the Silver Witch, and it was more for fun than for profit as Coyote never intervened or gave me clues. But everyone here at the Gold Star knew that when I showed up, it was going to be a high-stakes game.

And that I wouldn't be taking any prisoners.

"Mister Young!" The floor manager said coming up to me as I made my way towards the high-stakes tables in the back, "Your usual water?"

"Yes, please. Thank you, Umberto!"

"It's my pleasure, Paul!"

I couldn't help but smile, as I made my way to the one vacant seat that had suddenly opened up as I came over to the table. Pulling out ten thousand dollars I set it on the table as I sat down in the chair and looked up at the dealer, who was also smiling. Everyone here knew that I always tipped generously.

"Chips please, Scott."

"Sure thing, Paul."

It took me about fifteen minutes of playing to figure out just who my 'special friend' was tonight. I didn't know what they had done to provoke Coyote's ire, or why he felt they needed to learn a lesson. I'd given up looking into their pasts after the third one, as she and the previous two had most certainly deserved it.

Looking at the size of their chip stack, I would undoubtedly be here until the wee hours of the morning. I'd already picked up enough clues about them from the game so far to know that they wouldn't give up until they'd lost their last chip.

But then, they never did.

I had to smile and just shake my head at that. Grandmother would be pissed at my waking her up in the middle of the night. She still told me I was an unlucky bastard and that she felt sorry for me, but she never refused the money I'd hand over to her.

I had no idea at all what she did with it; that was her and Coyote's business. Though maybe one of these days I'd ask him just why he cared.

"Want to share the joke?" My new friend asked me, as I met his last bet.

"I used to work for the most unmerciful, deceitful, conniving and unforgiving bastard in the world. He got me stabbed, shot, poisoned, beat, you name it."

"So?"

"Yet, when he calls me up and asks for a favor, I'm out the door in a heartbeat!" I grinned at him, "Now, is that fucked up, or what?"

"Sounds like you've got some issues my friend," he replied checking his cards and placing another bet as the river card came out.

"I don't have issues," I laughed and raised him, "I have a subscription."

END

Afterword

First off I would like to say that if you enjoyed this book, I would be grateful if you could share that appreciation by giving the book a good rating, and a good review. If you want to see more stories from me like this, please check me out on Amazon, or go to my webpage at: **http://www.vanstry.net/**

For all of you who have been faithful fans, *thank you!* I appreciate you very much, and I do enjoy the occasional comment on my blog, facebook, or email. If you want to know when my next book is out, please sign up for my mailing list.

Writing this trilogy had some personal meaning for me. For one, I am part (though admittedly it is a very small part) American Indian. As a child we were told not to talk about it however, which was sad, because the people who knew the most of that part of our family history have long since passed on now that I'm an adult. So I've always wanted to do a story with a Native American aspect to it.

There were also a few things in this trilogy that actually happened in Real Life, either to me personally, or to people that I knew rather well (the non-magical things, of course!) Some of those things were minor, some were not-so-minor, and it felt good to mention them at long last somewhere, even if it was only in a fantasy story (and no, no hints!)

Again, thank you for buying and reading my books, I appreciate it tremendously, you folks have all been very kind to me and I'm very grateful for the opportunity to have shared these stories with you.

John Van Stry
www.vanstry.net - A list of all my books, and a freebie or two.
email: vanstry@gmail.com

Mailing list signup: **http://eepurl.com/2qrO9**

My Patreon page: **https://www.patreon.com/vanstry**

You can also find more of my stories on Amazon at:
http://www.amazon.com/John-Van-Stry/e/B004U7JY8I/

Made in the USA
Columbia, SC
24 August 2024